"IF THAT MOCKINGBIRD
DON'T SING . . ."

She placed the baby back in his crib. He was hers, hers to pamper and protect against the storm that raged outside her window.

He was sleeping now, and she pulled the rocking chair next to the crib and watched him.

"Momma's gonna buy you . . ." She couldn't remember the rest of the song.

No matter. He was her baby now. She'd killed to get him, and he was hers. There would be plenty of time for them to learn the words. He might even grow up and teach it to his brothers and sisters.

"You'd like that, wouldn't you, hon?" she said to the sleeping infant.

"If that mockingbird don't sing, Momma's gonna get you—a baby sister . . ."

THE LAST LULLABY

JESSE OSBURN

AN AVON FLARE BOOK

THE LAST LULLABY is an original publication of Avon Books. This work has never before appeared in book form. This work is a novel. Any similarity to actual persons or events is purely coincidental.

AVON BOOKS
A division of
The Hearst Corporation
1350 Avenue of the Americas
New York, New York 10019

Copyright © 1994 by Jesse Osburn
Published by arrangement with the author
Library of Congress Catalog Card Number: 93-90646
ISBN: 0-380-77317-1
RL: 5.8

First Avon Flare Printing: March 1994

AVON FLARE TRADEMARK REG. U.S. PAT. OFF. AND IN OTHER COUNTRIES, MARCA REGISTRADA, HECHO EN U.S.A.

Printed in the U.S.A.

RA   10   9   8   7   6   5   4   3   2

To Jim, Joan, Mary, and Woody . . .
my siblings, my friends

Prologue

"Hush, little baby, don't you cry . . ."

There was a clap of thunder, and the baby—her baby, whom she'd waited so long to hold in her arms—stirred.

Oh, please, don't wake up. "Hush, little baby . . ."

She'd planned everything so carefully. The back window, safe from the prying eyes of that nosy old neighbor woman. The exact number of steps to the baby's—her baby's—room. But she hadn't counted on the storm.

Another clap of thunder, another whimper from the baby. "Hush, little baby . . ."

She didn't want them to wake up. They'd try to stop her if they woke up, and they had no right. He was her baby. They were the two who kept her from what she wanted. It should have been her husband, her life, her baby.

But now the baby was starting to cry in earnest. Gently, she put him back in his crib. "Hush, little baby . . . I'll be right back. I just have to take care of something."

1

Tenderly, she stroked his smooth, pink cheek and ruffled his soft, brown hair. Her baby. She loved him so much.

She picked up the kitchen knife and headed toward the bedroom across the hall.

One

Swish! Swish!

Kim Delaney sat in the hospital parking lot as the car's wipers swept across the windshield in exact tempo to the rain. Her brother, Tim, was in the passenger seat, his elbow on the armrest, his eyes already closed. It had been a long day for all of them. Their mother had been in labor since early that morning and their father had never left her side, except once, to buy flowers in the florist shop downstairs. Tim had worked at the *Daily Script* until three o'clock, answering telephone calls and taking classified ads so Mrs. Pease was free to help the assistant editor get the paper out on time. Kim's dad owned New Testament's only newspaper and moonlighted as a crime scene photographer. The newspaper operation was a family affair. Kim and her brother worked there after school during the winter months and on alternate weekends in the summertime. Their work load would no doubt increase now that school was out and their mother would be on temporary leave of absence, though none of them knew exactly how long that would be. Tim had caught a ride to the hospital when he'd left the newspaper office and spent the rest of the day with his twin sister, pacing the floor.

Swish, the rain fell in sheets against the glass as Kim pulled out of the parking lot at ten minutes till midnight; swish, there was little the wipers could do to battle the torrential downpour or improve Kim's visibility as she drove down Second Thessalonians, headed toward Matthew Street. Beth Ann was still at the babysitter's; Kim hated to disturb her younger sister this late, to pull her out of a warm and comfortable bed and into the weather, but her mother insisted Beth Ann always slept better in her own bed and would be cranky all day tomorrow if she didn't wake up in familiar surroundings.

Kim tried to concentrate on the road, but the strain of trying to see beyond the glare of yellow headlights on the wet pavement gave her a headache within minutes. She found her thoughts slipping unwillingly back to the events of the day. She had a new baby sister. The love she already felt for Daphne was new and exciting; she couldn't remember feeling this near tears since the day Beth Ann was born. A baby . . . a miracle of birth . . . wasn't life wonderful?

She couldn't see more than a few feet in front of her as she turned west on Matthew and crossed the Psalm River Bridge. Luckily, there wasn't much traffic this time of night, not in this sleepy neighborhood.

Tim snored softly, his blond hair pushed back over his forehead, as his head sank farther and farther into the shadows that surrounded his side of the car.

She followed a slight curve in the road and hit the brakes without warning. Otherwise she would have rammed the back of her uncle's patrol car parked at an odd angle against the curb.

Tim jerked forward, instantly alert. "What is it?"

"I don't know."

He shielded his eyes from the flashing light; the red glare was especially harsh because of the rain and the puddles.

"Can you get through, Kim?"

"I don't know," she said again. A crowd of people stood motionless in the street, blocking traffic, unaware that she was even there.

She started to sound the horn, to let them know she wanted to pass, but there was something about the stillness of the crowd, the silence that surrounded the car—silent except for the pitter-patter of rain against the roof—that told her something tragic had happened on Matthew Street, and blaring her horn, making a noise of any kind, would seem irreverent.

"Maybe I ought to turn around," she said as she glanced over her shoulder. There was already another car behind her, blocking that direction, too.

"Don't you want to know what's going on?"

Tim often rode shotgun, with their Uncle Dare who was the town's police chief, or with one of his deputies because he wanted to pursue a career in law enforcement, not journalism, when he graduated high school. Kim knew from her brother's expression, and the way he was leaning forward in the car seat, that he was sorry he'd missed out on the action tonight.

Tim was rolling down his window, motioning to someone standing a few feet away. Kim couldn't tell if it was a man or a woman because of the bulky raincoat and the army-green hood pulled over their head.

Suddenly, Luke Levy appeared in front of the car, waving Kim forward as he backed through the crowd of people, making a path just wide enough for her to follow without hitting anyone.

"Hey, Luke! Deputy Levy!" Tim leaned out the window and cupped his hand over his mouth. "What's going on? Where's Uncle Dare?"

Luke removed a flashlight from his hip pocket and waved the beam of light toward the curb. Kim turned the steering wheel in that direction; the car was still moving when the deputy stuck his head inside Tim's window.

"What are you kids doing out so late?"

"We just came from the hospital. Mom had her baby," Tim answered.

"Where's your dad?"

"Still at the hospital. Why?"

"The Chief's been calling your house and leaving messages. Doesn't your dad carry a beeper anymore?"

"Sure." Kim leaned forward to see around her brother. "He turned it off today because—"

"Stay here." Luke had to shout to be heard above the raging wind. "I'll get your uncle." He darted back across the street before Kim or her brother could stop him.

Tim reached for the door handle. "What the heck's going on?"

Kim hated to leave the comfort of the car, the warm air that was blowing from the heater against her sneakered feet, but she, too, pushed open her door and stood with Tim at the fringes of the crowd. It had been a beautiful day, warm and sunny, when they'd gone to the hospital, so neither of them had worn a jacket.

Minutes later, Uncle Dare broke through the people gathered along the sidewalk shaking his head to a group of men who tried to question him.

"Luke says your momma's at the hospital. What'd we have?"

"A girl." Kim smiled proudly. "Daphne Nichole."

Her uncle smiled, too, but his acceptance of the good news was short-lived. "Can you call your dad? Tell him there's been a murder at

7

Matthew 727 and I need him to photograph the scene." He took Kim's arm gently in his hand and led her back toward the car. "I reached Mrs. Pease; she's trying to reach the assistant editor. But it's your dad I need."

"Murder?" Tim's voice had suddenly gone hoarse. He stared at the house, though all that was visible above the crowd was the top of the roof.

"Matthew 727," Kim said to her uncle. "That's David Sweet's house."

Uncle Dare's fingers tightened around Kim's arm suddenly, almost to the point of pain. "You knew him?"

"No." She shook her head. "Not really. Mr. Sweet came in Monday and subscribed to the paper. I remember his address because I wrote it down myself. He and his wife rented the Simpson place and moved in two weeks ago."

"Tell me." Her uncle raked his hand through his hair, his face ducked down to keep the rain out of his eyes. "Did he say anything about a baby?"

"Sure. He's practically all Mr. Sweet talked about."

"Get in the car, Kim." He grabbed her arm again and walked with her across the street. Jerking open the door, he waited until Kim was inside before he climbed into the back seat. Tim slammed his door closed seconds later.

"This is very important, Kim." She'd never seen her uncle more serious; as scared as she was about a murder in New Testament, she was more frightened that her mention of a baby had brought such a grim expression to her uncle's face.

"Tell me everything you know about the Sweets' baby," he said.

She blinked several times and tried to remember the conversation.

"He was born February 14th. I remember because Mr. Sweet made a joke about it being Valentine's Day."

"What else?"

"His name is Jason . . . or Jeremy. I'm sorry, Uncle Dare, I can't remember."

"What's this all about, Uncle Dare?" Tim asked.

Dare Delaney lowered his head again and rubbed his forehead with the heel of his hand. "Kids, we have a problem. I don't want to upset you, but you'll find out soon enough. The Sweets were murdered tonight. It looks like someone came in the window. Nothing appears to have been taken. Except for the baby. At least . . ." He looked up and Kim saw the raw terror in his eyes. The goose bumps that raced up and down her spine were the coldest she'd ever experienced, and she found herself shaking uncontrollably.

"Uncle Dare? What about the baby?"

"The baby is missing." He reached out and ran his hand down Kim's blond hair. "Are you sure, absolutely positive, that the Sweets had a baby and you're not confusing the man who came in the newspaper office with someone else?"

"I'm positive." Wasn't she? There was always the possibility that she'd made a mistake. She talked to a lot of people at the *Daily Script*. "It was David Sweet," she said with conviction. "And his son's name is Jeremy Don Sweet. I remember now."

"Okay." Her uncle's face was emotionless again. He reached for the door. "Call your dad. Tell him I need him ASAP."

"I'll call from Beth Ann's babysitter's house," Tim said.

"Maybe you two had better stay there tonight, too. Your parents would probably rest better knowing you weren't home alone. I know I would."

Kim nodded as her uncle left the car. She looked down at her hands; she'd been gripping the steering wheel so hard her fingers were drained of color.

"We'll leave Beth Ann at the babysitter's," Tim said. "You can stay there or I'll drive you home. But I'm coming back." He looked toward the house again and shook his head. "I can't believe I've been riding with Uncle Dare or Deputy Levy almost every night since school's been out and nothing's happened. Now this—"

"Tim." She looked over her shoulder at the house again. "Something like this isn't supposed to happen in New Testament."

Her brother looked down, studying his hands in silence. As disappointed as he was about missing out on the first part of the investigation, he realized there were two people dead, murdered in a house just a few feet away. Somehow the realization put them all—the whole town—in danger.

There was another blast of harsh light as a camera crew from KNTV began shooting footage of the bungalow and the neighbors milling about the street.

"What do you suppose happened to the Sweets' baby?" Kim asked. "Oh God, I hope he's okay."

"Hush, little baby, don't you cry. Momma's gonna buy you a mockingbird."

She placed her baby back in his crib and caressed his forehead once more, for her own peace of mind. He'd been feverish for almost an hour now and she was growing more concerned by the minute.

"If that mockingbird don't sing . . ."

He was the most precious child God had ever created, of that she had no doubt. And he was hers, her's to pamper and coo over and protect against the storm that raged outside her window.

She leaned over the bed and kissed the top of his head again. She loved the way he smelled, his tiny bottom softened with baby lotion, his tiny fingers rubbed with oil.

He was sleeping now, a bit too fitfully to please her so she pulled the rocking chair next to the crib and watched him silently for a few minutes, the only sounds in the nursery that of the baby's soft breathing and the chair runners as they creaked against the floor as gently as a lullaby.

"Momma's gonna buy you a . . ." She couldn't remember the rest of the song.

No matter. He was her baby now. There would be plenty of time for them to learn the words together. He might even grow up and teach it to his brothers and sisters.

"You'd like that, wouldn't you, hon?" she said to the sleeping infant. He twitched at the sound of her voice.

"If that mockingbird don't sing, Momma's gonna buy you . . . a baby sister."

Two

Wednesday, two days after the murders, Kim looked in on Daphne to make sure she was still sleeping peacefully before she went downstairs to make sandwiches for lunch. Tim and Beth Ann had gone to the movies soon after Daphne's arrival home from the hospital that morning. They were due home any minute.

Uncle Dare was seated at the table with Carol Delaney, his hands wrapped around a mug of steaming coffee. He'd stopped by to welcome Carol and Daphne home from the hospital. Today was the first time Kim had seen Uncle Dare since the night of the murders. He smiled and stopped talking the moment she entered the room.

"Don't mind me," she said as she went to the refrigerator and gathered sandwich makings from the top rack. "I know you're talking about the Sweets and I know you haven't caught their killer." She carried sliced ham, cheese, and a bowl of shredded lettuce to the counter and

13

grabbed a loaf of fresh bread from the cupboard. "Do you have any leads yet?"

"Lots of them." Uncle Dare usually loved to discuss his duties as chief of police but he was hesitant to involve his family in a murder investigation. Even Tim hadn't been allowed to ride with his uncle or the deputies since Monday night. "I think half of New Testament has a suspect in mind," he said wearily. "Brothers-in-law, ex-husbands, boyfriends. The problem is, nobody *knows* anything. It seems like the Sweets were virtually recluses. The neighbors had barely seen them, much less gotten to know them. Helen B. Ross, who doesn't miss anything that goes on in the neighborhood says they never even had any visitors."

"And you have to investigate every lead, of course?" Mrs. Delaney asked.

Dare nodded. "Luke Levy and Marsh Hampton are working overtime."

"Alex says there hasn't been a ransom demand for Jeremy Sweet. Maybe that's a good sign?"

Dare stared at his hands, nodding again, but not really answering.

"Do you think Jeremy's still alive?" Kim asked.

"Right now our investigation is based on a lot of assumptions and will be until we piece together all the facts." He paused, his coffee cup halfway to his mouth, and choosing his words carefully. "It's a safe bet whoever murdered the Sweets in their bed also took Jeremy.

14

I'm hoping he was taken by someone who will look after him, not someone who intends him harm."

Carol Delaney, always the optimist, forced herself to smile. "It seems to me the longer there's no ransom note, the more likely he's safe."

"Whoever murdered the Sweets is a violent person," Uncle Dare said. "There's no predicting what he or she might do in the future." His shoulders seemed to slump a little more as he finished his coffee and wrapped his fingers around the empty cup. "All I can do now is try to find Jeremy and return him to his grandparents where we'll know he'll be safe."

"How're you going to find him?" Kim asked as she put together the last sandwich and carried the platter, along with a bag of potato chips, to the table.

"I wish I knew. I've talked to David and Suzanne's families; naturally they're upset so it hasn't been easy doing a background check. The more I know about the victims' lives before they moved to New Testament, the more likely I am to come up with a motive for their murders. In the meantime, we've hand-delivered Jeremy's photograph to just about everybody in New Testament and surrounding communities. Alex agreed to run it on the front page every day. KNTV's doing a special report for a week. And it's been picked up by the wire services. Hopefully someone will see Jeremy, recognize him from all the publicity, and call us."

Suddenly the back door banged open and Beth Ann came bouncing in, a red balloon tied to her wrist. "Tim took me to the toy store after the movie since we were at the mall anyway. He bought me a balloon." She stood beside her mother's chair. "The movie was really boring. Tim wasn't going to buy Daphne a balloon because he says she's too little. But I made him anyway. Is Daphne asleep, Mommy?"

"Yes," Carol Delaney said. "So be very quiet when you go upstairs, okay?"

"Okay."

"And wash your hands before lunch." She brushed brown hair from Beth Ann's forehead and glanced up at Kim standing behind her uncle's chair. "There's something I need to tell you while we eat." It was an announcement she'd made to the twins the day before while she was still in the hospital, one Kim wasn't completely happy with though they'd discussed the details at length. "I've decided to go back to work at the newspaper sooner than planned." She was looking at Dare now, including him in the conversation. "I don't think Alex agrees completely with my decision, but the *Script* has such a small staff that one person being gone can make a big difference. The twins volunteered to work longer hours now that school's out, but I know Tim would rather be helping out at the police station, if it's okay with you, Dare."

He hesitated a moment, weighing his decision. "There's a lot of paperwork with the

Sweet case," he said finally. "Maybe Tim can help Rosy instead of riding with Luke or me. He knows how to handle himself in an emergency situation—it's the first thing I taught him—but I'd rather not take any unnecessary chances while there's a murder investigation going on."

"I offered to work full time at the newspaper," Kim said, "but Mom won't let me."

Her mother looked up and smiled. "I depend on you too much. Now that Daphne's home, we'll all be a little busier." She brushed Beth Ann's hair again and carried the empty cups to the sink. "Working at the *Script* doesn't leave you much time for a social life, Kim. I know you and Tim have plans with your friends this summer. I don't expect you to spend your entire vacation babysitting or answering phones at the *Script*." She returned to the table and spoke to Dare again. "That's why I've decided to hire a nanny and go back to work as early as next week."

"What's a nanny, Mommy?" Beth Ann asked.

"Someone to help me look after you and Daphne. I've already contacted an employment agency. Kim and I will start interviewing tomorrow afternoon."

Tim came through the back door, carrying a shopping bag in one hand and a pink balloon in the other. His face brightened the moment he saw Uncle Dare. "Anything new on the Sweet case?"

17

"I'll fill you in after lunch," Dare said, leaning back in his chair. "On our way back to the station."

Beth Ann raced around the table and tugged on her brother's sleeve. "Let's go upstairs and give Daphne her balloon."

"Remember, she's asleep," Carol Delaney said.

Uncle Dare rose from the table and followed them toward the stairs. "I think I'll have a look myself."

"Dare . . ." Kim's mother leaned against the counter, her arms folded. "You haven't told me what you think."

"About what?"

"About my going back to work." When he didn't respond immediately, she took a dish towel and dried her hands. "Maybe you can help me convince Alex it's not such a bad idea."

Dare grinned for the first time. "What? Going back to work? Or hiring a nanny?" His smile faded. "Alex is probably like everyone else in town. He can't stop thinking about what happened to the Sweets. Every time I see a baby, I look twice. I know it's not likely I'll run into Jeremy in the street, but that doesn't keep me from looking or hoping."

Kim saw the look that passed between her mother and her uncle and felt the weight of the Sweets' murders rest heavily on her shoulders, a bad dream that wouldn't go away. Like the rest of her family, she had been so wrapped up

18

in Daphne that today was the first time she had been reminded what Uncle Dare must have gone through since Monday night. Two people had been murdered and their infant son taken for no apparent reason. Not only did he have to worry about solving the Sweet case, he had to worry that something like this could happen again until he caught the killer.

"Dare . . ." Carol Delaney folded the dish towel and draped it across the hook above the sink. "When you talk to David Sweet's mother again, tell her . . . if there's anything I can do . . . I can't imagine what she must be going through. I think of her when I look at Daphne or Beth Ann. If anything ever happened to one of my children . . ."

"I'll tell her," Dare said and left the room.

Three

Thursday afternoon Kim was dressed in her best jeans and favorite sweater, hoping to impress Barbara Chancellor, the fifth nanny the employment agency had sent over that day. Later, she realized she needn't have bothered. Miss Chancellor spent the first thirty minutes ignoring her, not even acknowledging Kim was in the room.

Barbara Chancellor, with her blond hair pulled back in a chignon, sat on the living room sofa, her leather purse clutched firmly in her lap, a cup and saucer on the table beside her. She had insisted her tea be prepared a certain way—with honey instead of sugar—and then refused to drink it because it was too sweet. When Kim volunteered to pour another cup, the nanny had answered Carol Delaney instead. "I'd just as soon forget tea and get on with the interview. I have other appointments this afternoon."

Kim sat in the leather wingback opposite the

sofa and steeled herself for a lengthy session of questions. Miss Chancellor might have been the most qualified of he candidates so far, and the most highly recommended from her former employers, but her manners were a little too brusque, her attitude a little too haughty to suit Kim. She was almost certain Beth Ann wouldn't like her either.

"I understand from the agency that you have a newborn," Miss Chancellor said. "I'd like to meet her. Now, if it's convenient."

Carol Delaney hesitated for just a moment. "Kim, would you mind?" she said finally, motioning toward the stairs. "It's about time for Daphne to be waking up anyway." She smiled, hoping the nanny would take her lead and relax, perhaps even smile herself. "I'm sure she'll be starving. Daphne has a terrific appetite."

Miss Chancellor stared straight ahead, her expression unchanged.

Kim slipped quietly from the room. When she opened the nursery door a few moments later, Daphne was looking around, her soft blue eyes heavy with sleep, her cheeks as rosy pink as the blanket that covered her.

"Hi, angel." Kim carried her sister to the changing table, the same one her mother had used with Beth Ann. "You're right on schedule, as always."

In the short time Daphne had been home from the hospital, she had set a schedule which Kim and the rest of the family had adjusted to quickly. She napped at the same times, she seldom cried except when she was hungry, and—her mother was right—Daphne had an appetite that surprised everyone.

Kim couldn't help but smile as she changed her sister's diaper. Daphne was such a sweet baby, and though she was still too young to do much of anything except eat and sleep, she was definitely a Delaney. So like her mother and father, and even Beth Ann at times. But Daphne had a personality all her own, too. Kim knew other people might tease her if they knew what she was thinking. How could a baby only a few days old be all that Kim imagined her to be? She still remembered how she felt the first time she'd seen her sister at the hospital, less than an hour after she'd been born. It seemed so long ago now, so much had happened. But Kim had felt something stir in her heart, emotions she'd never experienced before, not even with Beth Ann. Daphne was going to grow up to be strong and sweet, probably less rambunctious than Beth Ann. She'd probably be quiet spoken like her father, a bookworm like her mother, and she'd want to work with Kim at the *Daily Script* until she was old enough to move on to bigger places, bigger publications. Perhaps someday she'd be a top reporter in Chicago or New York. Kim could imagine it now, her sister, her baby sister, accepting a Pulitzer Prize. . . .

Daphne cooed loudly and kicked her tiny feet, jarring Kim back to reality. She worked quickly replacing Daphne's cotton gown with a dress from the top drawer, never taking her eyes from her sister, not even for one second.

Her thoughts had taken another turn, one that frightened her so badly, she was afraid to admit to herself what she was thinking. How often had Suzanne Sweet changed Jeremy's diapers, just the way Kim was doing now? How often had she dreamed wonderful dreams for her son? Had she hoped for Jeremy what Kim hoped for her sister . . . a wonderful life with wonderful, rewarding experiences? Of course she had. What mother didn't?

Kim felt the happiness of a few minutes ago replaced with a sadness she couldn't push back no matter how hard she tried. Suzanne Sweet was dead, her son missing. Just a few days ago they had been a family, the three of them. Though Kim had met David Sweet only briefly, she recognized all the signs of a man who loved his son more than he could ever say in words. He'd handed Jeremy's photograph to Kim across the front counter of the *Script* and introduced him as the future president of the United States. Kim had laughed then; she felt like crying now. The tragedy had struck so suddenly, the killings had been so senseless.

Daphne gurgled again and turned her head, brushing her cheek against Kim's fingers. Kim lifted the infant to her shoulder and rested her hand gently but firmly to support her sister's head. Thinking about the Sweets made her love Daphne even more. And Beth Ann, too.

Her sisters were so young, so innocent. Thank goodness they were too young to realize the full impact of what had happened on Matthew Street just a few nights ago.

She carried Daphne to the door, whispering a silent prayer for Jeremy Don Sweet and another, more urgent one for her sisters.

Downstairs, Kim heated a bottle and draped a towel over her shoulder so Daphne wouldn't spit up on her favorite sweater. When they entered the living room a few minutes later, Barbara Chancellor rose immediately to her feet. The hard lines that had been etched around her eyes and at the corners of her mouth faded quickly, replaced by a smile so unexpected it made Kim stop halfway between the door and her mother's chair.

"Oh, such a tiny thing." Miss Chancellor's voice had changed, too, softened somehow, as if she was afraid of speaking too loudly now that Daphne was in the room.

"Aren't you precious?" She stepped around the coffee table and walked to Kim so quickly, Kim didn't have time to react. "You're more beautiful than I imagined."

She took Daphne suddenly, lifting her from Kim's grasp so gently that it was a few seconds before Kim realized the pressure she felt against her shoulder was no longer Daphne's head, but the towel.

"Miss Chancellor was just telling me a little about herself, where she grew up, where she went to school, things like that." Carol

24

Delaney raised her eyebrows when Kim looked her direction. She shrugged her shoulders as if to say she knew exactly how Kim felt. Neither of them liked the idea of Daphne being handled by strangers, especially one who hadn't asked permission first. "I was just about to tell her what a handful Beth Ann can be sometimes. Hopefully she won't withdraw her application once I finish."

"We're going to get along just fine." Miss Chancellor looked up. "May I?" she asked, indicating the bottle in Kim's hand.

Kim looked at her mother and reluctantly handed the bottle to the nanny.

Mrs. Delaney studied the typed references Barbara Chancellor had given her when she'd first arrived. "I see from your work history you've never babysat anyone under four years old."

Miss Chancellor looked up, frowning. "I am not a babysitter, Mrs. Delaney." Her voice, though still soft spoken, did nothing to hide her displeasure. "I am a nanny. There is a difference."

She sat on the sofa again and held the bottle while Daphne suckled noisily. "While it's true my charges have all been older than your daughter, you'll note I've been trained to care for children of all ages, including infants." Her gaze was fixed solidly on Daphne though her words were directed to Mrs. Delaney. "Daphne will be as safe in my care as anyone else you might hire. More so, probably."

25

"I didn't mean to imply—"

"I do hope you'll give me the opportunity to be a nanny to Daphne." Miss Chancellor looked up finally and smiled, this time including Kim. "I love all children, but there's a special place in my heart for newborns."

"As you know I'm looking for someone who can do a little light housekeeping in addition to seeing after my daughters." Mrs. Delaney passed the references to Kim before she continued. "I told you this morning on the telephone that Kim is wonderful when it comes to helping out. I rarely have to ask, she usually knows exactly what to do."

"Yes." Miss Chancellor looked at Kim and tried to act impressed, though it was obvious to them both that she wasn't. "Of course."

"My husband and I have a newspaper to run. It takes both of us working full time."

"I understand." Miss Chancellor placed the bottle on the coffee table and lifted Daphne to her shoulder, patting her back ever so gently. "When I do I get to meet Beth Ann?"

"I asked Tim—that's my son—to take her to the park this afternoon. Beth Ann can be a bit rambunctious at times. I wanted to make sure we could talk without any interruptions."

Miss Chancellor finally looked at Kim. "Why didn't you take her to the park? I mean, since you're so good with her."

Kim was caught off guard by the question. She straightened up in the chair and met Miss Chancellor's stare with one of her own. "I stayed to meet you, of course."

"Hiring someone so I could go back to work was a family decision," Carol Delaney said. "I asked Kim to sit in on the interviews because I trust her judgment."

The clock on the fireplace mantel chimed three o'clock. Miss Chancellor rose from the sofa a few minutes later, reluctantly, and handed Daphne back to Kim. "You have my resumé. Your mother can tell you what questions I answered while you were upstairs. I'm sure you'll make the right decision when it comes time to hiring a nanny." She retrieved her purse and moved toward the foyer. "You have my number, Mrs. Delaney."

"I'll call the agency. They'll let you know my decision."

"Thank you." Miss Chancellor paused long enough to glance back at Daphne. "You have a beautiful family, Mrs. Delaney. I'll look after them, care for them, and love them as if they were my own. Please remember that when reviewing my qualifications."

"I will. Thank you."

Kim was still in the living room a few minutes later, Daphne cradled in her lap, fighting sleep, when her mother returned from walking Miss Chancellor to the porch.

"Well, Kim, what'd you think?"

"She's . . ." Kim hesitated. She didn't want to be overly critical. So far none of the nannies they'd interviewed had been overly impressive. Most of them had been too young and too inexperienced. Barbara Chancellor was two years older than her mother and had spent most of her adult life employed by families who sang her praises. All but one said they would hire her again if given the opportunity. The Delaneys were lucky someone of Miss Chancellor's qualifications had moved to New Testament recently. Still, there was something about the woman's demeanor that troubled Kim. She was just too . . . pushy was the only word that occurred to Kim on such short notice.

"She's no-nonsense," her mother said as she gathered up the tea service and headed toward the kitchen. "Maybe that's what Beth Ann needs. Someone to make her toe the line. You and Tim spoil her rotten."

Kim smiled. It was true. "I don't think Miss Chancellor has a sense of humor though." She followed her mother to the kitchen, Daphne asleep in her arms.

"It certainly seems that way." Carol Delaney was busily preparing for their next interview in twenty minutes. It was their last scheduled appointment. Kim's mother wanted to make a decision that evening so she could contact the employment agency first thing in the morning. The new nanny, whoever she might be, would begin work Monday morning at eight o'clock.

"As it stands, Barbara Chancellor seems the most likely candidate." Mrs. Delaney stood at the sink with her back to Kim. "She has more experience than any of the other applicants.

She seems a bit standoffish, not quite what I expected from someone who works with young children on a daily basis. A few days with Beth Ann ought to cure that."

Kim left her mother downstairs fluffing the throw pillows on the living room sofa and carried Daphne upstairs to the nursery. She hadn't realized until now, when it was almost time to make a final decision, just how difficult it would be to choose her sisters' nanny. When it came to Beth Ann and Daphne's best interests she had to put aside her tastes in personality (most of the women had been friendly and outgoing save Miss Chancellor) and vote for the most qualified candidate. Maybe Miss Chancellor had just been nervous, uncomfortable being interviewed. Kim dismissed the idea immediately. The woman had been cold, distant and unfriendly on purpose. The only show of genuine emotion was when she'd held Daphne and fed her her bottle.

And who could blame her? Daphne was beautiful; whose heart wouldn't melt at the sight of her? Kim smiled as she placed her sister in the crib and watched over her for a few minutes longer. Miss Chancellor had promised to care for Beth Ann and Daphne, to love them as if they were her own. That was more than any of the others had promised.

The doorbell rang at ten minutes till four. Kim left the door to Daphne's room open and went downstairs to help her mother conduct the last of their interviews.

That night, after supper, Tim was seated across the booth in the New Testament Diner, his elbows on the table, his chocolate sundae untouched, most of the ice cream melted into a puddle of brown. He was staring out the window, watching the cars that traveled past. It was still too light outside for most of the drivers to have turned on their headlights.

"What's with you?" Kim asked. "You haven't heard a word I've said since we got here."

Tim turned his attention back to his sister and forced himself to smile. "I was just thinking about Uncle Dare."

Kim sipped her strawberry malt. "What about Uncle Dare?"

"The Sweet case is the most exciting thing that's happened in New Testament in a long time and he won't even let me be part of it." Tim stared at his hands for a moment, deep in thought. "I mean, I'm not glad it happened or anything like that. I'm sorry the Sweets were murdered. But the truth is, I want to know what's going on in the investigation and Uncle Dare will barely discuss it with me."

"You're just sorry he won't let you ride shotgun anymore," Kim said matter-of-factly.

Tim nodded. "I was looking forward to this summer. But now . . ." His voice trailed off as he stared out the window again. "I know working with Rosy's important, I guess I should be glad Uncle Dare will let me do at least that much. But it's not the same, you know?"

Kim didn't answer. She knew her twin well enough to know he didn't expect a response. All he wanted was a sympathetic ear, someone to share his thoughts with, and it didn't matter whether Kim agreed or not.

She stared across the table for a few moments, watching her brother closely. They'd decided to come to the diner, hoping some of their friends might be there. Kim hadn't seen Debra Harding, her best friend, in several days, not since before Daphne was born. She'd started to telephone Debra before leaving the house, but Tim had hurried her out of the house before she'd had a chance.

She looked around the brightly-lit room. There were several kids from East James High, all of them she knew by name, but none of them were close friends. She'd stopped by one table to talk for a few minutes when she'd first arrived, but Tim had gone immediately to the booth. She was glad now she hadn't lingered long. All anyone wanted to talk about was the Sweets' murders and ask questions about her uncle's investigation. She loved Uncle Dare, but sometimes being the niece of the chief of police could be a burden.

"Uncle Dare's under a lot of pressure to find Jeremy Sweet," Tim said. "I wish he would."

Kim nodded in silent agreement. She knew enough about police work to know the killer might not be identified for weeks, months, or maybe not at all. But a missing four-month-old made her uncle's job that much more stressful.

31

Not only did he have to cooperate with state and federal agencies, he had to answer to the mayor of New Testament and everyone who lived there. Jeremy Don was in danger as long as he was missing; no one felt safe as long as there was a killer free.

"I worry about Daphne."

She hadn't realized she had spoken the words aloud until Tim turned away from the window with a puzzled expression.

"Why?" he asked.

She shrugged, not really knowing the answer. She felt a protectiveness for Daphne that she couldn't remember having when Beth Ann was born. But then a young couple hadn't been murdered, their son abducted, either.

"Is it because Mom and Dad decided to hire a nanny?" Tim asked.

She shrugged again. "Maybe. I'm not sure I like the idea of a stranger spending so much time with Daphne and Beth Ann. You've worked at the *Script* enough to know what can happen, you've read the stories that come over the wire service. Child abuse, neglect, kidnappings. One baby's been taken in New Testament, it could happen again."

Tim stared out the window for a moment. Finally, he turned back, not so serious as before. "Mom spent most of the afternoon on the telephone following up on Miss Chancellor's references. I even heard her talking to Miss Chancellor again, asking more questions."

Kim had been upstairs with Beth Ann during the conversations, but her mother had informed the rest of the family during dinner that she thought hiring Miss Chancellor was the best solution. None of the other applicants had her experience, nor did any of them come as highly recommended. Kim hadn't agreed right away—she just couldn't forget how unpersonable Miss Chancellor had been that afternoon—and she thought for a moment that her mother might change her mind, too. But in the end, Kim agreed with everyone else and the decision was made. Barbara Chancellor would start to work for the Delaneys at eight o'clock on Monday morning.

"Daphne's going to be fine. Beth Ann, too." Tim turned his attention back to his sundae, eating it hurriedly, though most of the ice cream had already melted. "Nothing bad's going to happen. Honest."

Kim stared out the window, watching as a stream of headlights passed in front of the diner. She couldn't help but wonder if David Sweet had ever made the same promise.

Four

Barbara Chancellor started to work as scheduled. Kim had had time to think about the new nanny, to decide that maybe she'd been unfair the first time they'd met. Miss Chancellor had been unfriendly, ignoring Kim for the most part, but maybe all she needed was a little time to warm up to working for the Delaneys.

By Tuesday morning—just twenty-four hours later—Kim was positive that her first impression had been right.

"I can't believe you're letting her do this," she said as her mother poured her second cup of coffee.

Carol Delaney looked up from the counter, surprised. "Honestly, Kim, don't you think you're overreacting?" She carried her cup to her desk in the corner of the kitchen and opened the top drawer. "Miss Chancellor only made a list of duties for you and Tim and a daily schedule for Beth Ann." Her mother checked the batteries in her tape recorder before hurrying toward the door.

She hadn't planned to return to work for another week but there was an emergency city council meeting at nine o'clock, one which she insisted she cover for the newspaper since all the other staff members, including Mrs. Pease, had other obligations which couldn't be ignored. Kim's father hadn't been happy as he'd rushed out the door. His wife deserved more time off. Miss Chancellor needed supervision the first few days. . . . But Carol Delaney had insisted she'd only be gone for a short time, just long enough to sit in on the meeting and return to the news office in order to write up her notes. The assistant editor could finalize the story for publication.

"It's about time we had a little organization in this family," Kim's mother said as she glanced around the room, in a hurry to leave, but wanting to make sure she hadn't forgotten anything. "What's the big deal?" she asked, looking at Kim again.

"I'll tell you what the big deal is . . ." Kim began, but her mother was already hurrying toward the door again.

Daphne was over a week old and the Delaneys had returned to their normal schedule. That meant one or both of her parents rushing off to work first thing in the morning. Sometimes publishing a newspaper seemed like nothing more than one continuous deadline.

Kim returned to the laundry room, muttering to herself, and stared at the typewritten pages taped to the wall above the dryer. This was Miss Chancellor's second day at work and she was already taking control of their lives.

"I didn't know she was my nanny, too."

She read her list of duties—make her bed every morning, carry her own laundry downstairs and make sure there were no wet towels left in the bathroom. No matter how hard she tried, she couldn't help but feel frustrated that Miss Chancellor had dominion over her daily routine. These were things she did anyway. She didn't need a nanny reminding her to clean up after herself.

What truly irked her was Beth Ann's schedule. Between reading time in the morning and quiet time in the afternoon—and a long list of other activities all supervised by Miss Chancellor—there was little time left for Kim to spend with her sister.

Tim padded into the kitchen, dressed in his pajamas, and barefoot. His blond hair was tousled from a night of sleep. "What're you reading?"

"Haven't you heard?" she asked, glancing over her shoulder. "Mom and I hired a drill sergeant instead of a nanny."

"Beth Ann said something about a list of chores." Tim scratched his head and looked around the kitchen drowsily. "What's the first thing I have to do before I can have breakfast?"

"Did you make your bed?"

"Yes."

"Did you carry your dirty laundry downstairs?"

He looked down at his pajamas and grinned. "I'm wearing my dirty laundry."

Kim left her brother in the kitchen, pouring himself a bowl of cereal, and headed upstairs to the nursery. Schedule or no schedule, she always spent a few minutes with Daphne before her sister's bath.

Miss Chancellor, dressed in a gray dress and heavy black shoes that were designed for comfort, not style blocked the doorway to Daphne's room. Her blond hair was tied into a tight bun. "Now's not a good time," she said leaving no room for argument. "Daphne's not used to having me around yet. Your presence is, frankly, a distraction, Kim."

She closed the door so suddenly Kim had to step back to avoid being hit. Seconds later, the lock slid into place.

"She locked the door, Mother!"

Carol Delaney looked up from her desk at the *Daily Script*. It was just after eleven-thirty and she was hurrying to finish a rough draft of the council meeting so she could get home in time to help Miss Chancellor with lunch.

"What's the real problem here, Kim? I thought we all agreed we needed an extra hand." She sat in front of the computer, her hands poised on the keyboard. "Have you had a change of heart?"

"No." Kim paused a moment to consider the question. She hadn't changed her mind about hiring a nanny. But she hadn't changed her mind about Miss Chancellor either. She hadn't liked her in the beginning and she didn't like her now. "I think we hired the wrong woman," she said flatly.

Her mother looked down at her notes again, decided the conversation was more important and leaned back in her chair, resigned to handle one problem at a time. "Why is that?"

"I don't like being told when I can see my sisters."

Her mother nodded in agreement. "Miss Chancellor is a bit too authoritative. Even your father said so on his way out the door this morning. But maybe in a week or two—"

"A week or two!" Kim had a lot more in common with her father than just his blond hair and blue eyes. When there was a problem she wanted immediate action. "I don't think I can wait that long. Miss Chancellor made me so mad this morning I wanted to bust down the door."

Her mother removed her reading glasses and rubbed the bridge of her nose. "Remember, Kim, she needs time to adjust, too. Miss Chancellor has never worked in a household with teenage children."

"But she's so—"

"You sat through the interviews. You know she's the most qualified."

Kim was fighting a losing battle and she knew it. Miss Chancellor was qualified, highly qualified, and no amount of arguing on Kim's part would change her mother's mind. Carol Delaney wasn't about to do anything as rash as fire someone she'd just hired.

What was the harm in waiting a few more days? Maybe Miss Chancellor would lighten up once she realized she wasn't running a boot camp. Given the chance, Kim could prove just how helpful she could be around the house, especially with her sisters. Maybe then things would change.

"You know what I think the real problem is?" her mother asked. "I think you have too much free time now that school's out. I know you'd like to spend more time here, at the office, but frankly I'd like to see you pursue other interests this summer. If you expect to be a good journalist, you have to get out and experience new things, meet new people."

Kim was instantly alert for trouble. She knew when she was about to be talked into doing something she didn't want to do.

"I overheard Mrs. Pease talking on the telephone when I came in. Christian County Memorial Hospital is begging for volunteers."

Kim watched her mother carefully. "What kind of volunteers?"

"They've had so many cutbacks lately you could probably choose your own job. Mrs. Pease is friends with the director; why don't you ask her to set up an appointment?" She glanced at the clock over the front door. "If you ask her now, I'll bet you can get in this afternoon."

"Are you saying you don't want me to work at the newspaper anymore?" Kim already knew the answer but she had to ask anyway. Her mother knew how much Kim loved working at the *Daily Script*, and she'd never ask her daughter to give up something so important.

"Your father and I depend on you, we always have. But there's not a whole lot you can do until Mrs. Pease goes on vacation. And that's not until the end of summer." Her mother replaced her glasses and smiled reassuringly. "I'm just asking that you try something new, at least for a while. Just until we've given Miss Chancellor a fair chance. I promise, if things don't improve, I'll talk to her. Okay?"

Kim nodded. Her mother was already involved in her notes, her fingers moving steadily across the keys, by the time she approached Mrs. Pease's desk and asked her to contact the volunteer director.

Kim arrived at Christian County Memorial Hospital ten minutes before her appointment. She was in a better mood than she had been that morning, especially since she'd managed to go home and change into something more suitable for meeting the director without another confrontation with Miss Chancellor. She'd even managed to sneak a peek at Daphne, who had been sleeping, her angelic face softened by the shadows that filled the nursery.

Kim had barely had time to settle herself in one of the overstuffed chairs in the lobby, being careful not to wrinkle her white skirt and pink blouse before Evelyn Davis came out to greet her.

"I'm so glad your mother told you about our program." Mrs. Davis, with her white hair carefully coiffured and her yellow-and-white smock designating her as a hospital volunteer, sat in a chair beside Kim and talked as easily as if they were old friends. Evelyn Davis was a widow, her children were all married and moved away from New Testament. She had volunteered at the hospital three years ago and just last week been named Director of Volunteers. "Have you ever been to the hospital before, Kim?"

"Never as a patient."

"Thank goodness for that." Mrs. Davis looked around the lobby and smiled. It was obvious how much she liked her work and how glad she was that the volunteer program was part of Christian County Memorial.

"My sisters were born here," Kim said after a few moments of silence. "Beth Ann five years ago and Daphne just last week."

"Daphne Delaney. Of course, I remember." The older woman's smile faded quickly. "That was the same night those poor people were murdered on Matthew Street, wasn't it?"

"Yes, ma'am." Kim looked away quickly, running her hand over her skirt to smooth away imaginary wrinkles. She hated to think that one of the happiest days of her life would always be associated with one of New Testament's biggest tragedies.

"Let me take you on a tour of the hospital." Mrs. Davis held Kim's arm as they walked to the elevators. "We'll go to the third floor first. I think you'd be perfect working in our library. Though it's hardly a library at all." She waited until Kim was in the elevator before pushing the button to the top floor. "We distribute reading material, mostly magazines, to our patients twice daily, once in the morning and again in the afternoon. It's a wonderful way to meet the patients. Do you think you'd like that?"

"Yes, ma'am. I think so." Mrs. Davis's enthusiasm was contagious. For the first time Kim was glad she'd followed her mother's suggestion. Working at the hospital would give her an opportunity to get out of the house and avoid Miss Chancellor. Plus it would be a new experience, a way to meet people. She might even write a series of articles about the volunteer program and submit them for publication in the *Daily Script* or the *East James High Jamboree*.

"Some of our patients are lonely," Mrs. Davis said. "They like someone to talk to."

She chatted amiably and pointed out several points of interest once they stepped off the elevator on the third floor—the storage closet where two metal carts with reading materials were stored and a box near the nurses' station where people dropped off donated books and magazines. Kim was introduced to several of the hospital employees. They were all friendly, though most of them were too overworked to spend much time visiting with a new volunteer.

Before long they were back in the elevator again, riding down to the second floor. The nursery was located in the west wing.

"I come here every day to look at the newborns," Mrs. Davis said. "As of this morning we had two girls and three boys. The employees break room is just around the corner." She pointed to her left as they stepped off the elevator. "There are vending machines. Soft drinks. Gum. Candy."

By the time they finished their tour of the north and south wings, Kim felt as if she had been friends with Evelyn Davis for a long time. She knew the names and ages of her grandchildren, where they lived and where they went to school. She knew Mrs. Davis was seeing one of the doctors socially, though Mrs. Davis refused to call it dating. They'd dined together several times and attended a bluegrass festival in Mill Creek, a town forty miles away.

Eventually they reached the nursery. Kim paused in front of the plate glass window. The night Daphne was born came back in vivid detail, the way her mother had suffered with every contraction but refused to admit she was in pain, the way her father had paced the floor but refused to admit he was nervous. Tim had sat in a corner of the room trying to act nonchalant, but he had been the first one to race to the telephone to call his friends when the news finally came that it was a girl.

Kim was so lost in her memories she hardly noticed when Mrs. Davis excused herself to go to the ladies room. She didn't know how long she had been staring through the window at the newborns before she was interrupted.

"Cute, aren't they?"

She turned and looked at the young, blond nurse standing beside her.

"Millie Thorne," the woman said, extending her hand.

"Kim Delaney." Millie's handshake was firm, friendly. "I'm a new volunteer."

"Do you like babies?"

"Of course."

"I could tell by your expression." Millie smiled, turning her attention back to the infants. Some were sleeping, others were being attended to by the nurses on duty. Only one was crying.

"I was just thinking about the last time I was here," Kim said when the silence stretched out. "Last week. My sister was born."

"What's her name? Maybe I was on duty."

"Daphne Delaney."

44

Millie thought for a moment and shook her head. "I don't remember the name. Do you have a picture?"

"I . . ."

"Hello, Millie." Mrs. Davis returned from the ladies room. "I see you've met our newest volunteer."

"Yes." She checked her watch. "It's almost three o'clock, time for my shift to begin. I'll see you around, Kim." She walked away, her white shoes squeaking against the tile floor.

"You'll meet most of our staff," Mrs. Davis said. "I think you'll find them all nice as Millie." She took Kim's arm again and walked with her to the elevator. "Let's go to my office, dear, and we'll work out a schedule. As desperate as we are for volunteers, I'll let you pick out what days you want to work and I'll even let you chose your own hours. How's that sound?"

Working for Mrs. Davis was going to be better than she expected. She'd still have time to spend at the *Daily Script* working with her parents, and her evenings would be free to spend with her sisters once Miss Chancellor went home at the end of the day.

Kim smiled as the elevator doors closed.

Her mind was already racing with story ideas for her first article.

Five

Kim avoided Miss Chancellor whenever she could. The new nanny continued to enforce her rules with an iron fist. Every day Kim found some new task added to her list taped to the laundry room wall. Beth Ann complained about her daily regime, but only to Kim, never to her mother, and certainly not to the nanny. Kim's mother seemed to be the only member of the family who got along with the nanny. By Thursday afternoon, the fourth day Miss Chancellor had worked for the family, she and Carol Delaney were downstairs in the kitchen giggling over some magazine article like old friends.

Kim resigned herself to spending time with her sisters after six when Miss Chancellor went home for the evening. She went immediately to the nursery after dinner and always stopped by again for a few minutes on her way to bed. Her sister was usually asleep by then; Kim would stand silently by the crib and watch as Daphne slept. She seemed to grow and change every day. Her hair had grown darker, thicker, as brown as Beth Ann's. Her eyes were as blue as ever.

Sometimes Tim would peek in on his way to his room, but he never lingered long if Kim was there. She knew he sometimes stayed for hours if no one else was around. Occasionally she heard him behind the closed door cooing and talking the most inane baby talk. They had a lot in common, she and Tim. Tim was as crazy about Daphne as Kim was, although he'd sooner die than admit it.

Friday morning Kim was dressed and downstairs for breakfast by nine o'clock. She had worked at the hospital Wednesday, the day after her meeting with Mrs. Davis, and was scheduled to return today at noon. Mrs. Davis had eagerly accepted her schedule—Mondays, Wednesdays and Fridays from noon till four— and posted her hours on a bulletin board beside her office door.

Tim was seated at the table, just finishing breakfast, when Kim entered the room. He looked up, smiled and nodded toward a platter of scrambled eggs, bacon, and homemade biscuits. "Miss Chancellor's reward for doing our chores so well." Until today she'd never cooked breakfast, only lunch and dinner.

Kim poured herself a glass of orange juice and joined her brother at the table. Tim was

47

dressed, waiting for Luke Levy to pick him up and drive him to the station.

"What's new on the Sweet case?" she asked, staring at the food and deciding she wasn't hungry. She'd eat something later in the hospital cafeteria.

Tim shrugged. "Nothing." He took one more bite, decided he'd had enough and pushed his plate away. "Nothing earth shattering, that is. Uncle Dare is still questioning the Sweets' friends, people they knew in California. He spent the last two days on the telephone with David Sweet's college buddies. I heard him asking one guy about Mr. Sweet's social life, where he hung out, who he dated, things like that."

Kim drank her orange juice and decided not to ask any more questions. Every time she thought about the Sweets, especially Jeremy, she felt an empty ache in her stomach that wouldn't go away. Her father had assured her that Uncle Dare and everyone else was doing everything possible to locate the missing boy, but it seemed the more time that passed the less convinced her father sounded that everything was going to turn out for the best. Jeremy Don Sweet had been missing for nearly two weeks, and though several people reported seeing a baby who fit his description, the leads had turned out to be dead ends. She knew how frustrating the investigation must have been for her uncle. But she couldn't stop thinking about herself either, how she felt each time she looked at Daphne and tried not to think about how easy Jeremy had been taken, and the danger he was in.

Pushing her chair away from the table, she headed toward the door, the stairs leading to Daphne's room.

"Where're you going?" Tim asked, surprised at her sudden departure.

"I forgot something upstairs," she lied. She couldn't tell him the truth, couldn't admit even to herself that she had a sudden urge to see her little sister, to hold her in her arms and cradle her head against her shoulder. Daphne was so young, so innocent; every minute Kim could spend with her seemed more precious than the last.

Miss Chancellor was upstairs with the nursery door locked. Kim knocked quietly, just in case Daphne was still asleep, though she knew it was past the time for her bath. Miss Chancellor followed Daphne's schedule as rigidly as she did everyone else's.

She knocked again, louder this time. A few seconds later she heard footsteps, and then Miss Chancellor's voice.

"Yes?"

"It's Kim, Miss Chancellor. May I see Daphne please?"

"I'm dressing her just now. Is there a reason you wanted to see her, Kim?"

"No reason." Kim fought to keep the impatience from her voice. She'd promised herself to avoid any confrontations with Miss Chancellor. At any costs. "Why do you have the door locked, Miss Chancellor?"

"Beth Ann," she said, as if that explained everything.

"What about Beth Ann?"

Kim could hear the nanny sigh heavily, even through the closed door. "Do you mind if we discuss this later, Kim? Daphne is only half dressed and I'm afraid she might catch a chill if I don't hurry."

Her footsteps away from the door marked the end of the conversation.

Kim lingered outside for a few moments longer with no way to express her anger. Miss Chancellor had her locked out, her mother would insist she was making a mountain out of a molehill, and Tim was leaving for the police station. She listened as he went out the front door, and the house grew silent again. Silent except for the muffled sound of Beth Ann's voice in her room at the end of the hall. Beth Ann and Carol Delaney were reading a book together, a rare treat for both of them since Mrs. Delaney no longer had to rush off to work every morning.

Kim decided to let the matter drop for now. Tomorrow was Saturday, the start of the weekend, which meant two days without Miss Chancellor. She could see Daphne whenever she wanted and she wouldn't have to feel like an intruder in her own house.

* * *

Kim arrived at Christian County Memorial, donned her yellow-and-white smock and began distributing books and magazines to the patients on the second floor at a few minutes past noon.

She saw Millie Thorne ten minutes later, at the end of the hall, near the maternity ward, but they were both too busy to visit. It wasn't until the end of her four-hour shift, when she was preparing to go home, that Kim met her again. Millie was standing by the bank of elevators in the upstairs waiting room as Kim pushed the cart of reading materials toward the storage closet.

Millie's blond hair was plaited in a single braid that hung down her back, the end tied with a white ribbon. She looked up at the sound of the metal cart. "Hello, Kim."

"Hello, Millie. How are you?"

She shrugged, pushing impatiently at the elevator button. "So-so. How do you like your new job?"

Kim leaned against the cart to take some weight off her feet; she wasn't accustomed to so much exercise. The metal cart was heavier than it looked and the wheels tended to make a lot of noise, occasionally getting stuck, refusing to budge no matter how hard she pushed. The countless trips she made up and down the hospital corridors in her good dress shoes were beginning to take their toll on her ankles.

"Mrs. Davis says I'm doing a good job." She glanced down at the cart, the magazines and periodicals stacked neatly on the top rack, novels and non-fiction books on the space below. "She says the patients appreciate what I'm doing."

"I'm sure they do." Millie jabbed at the elevator button again. Both cars were stuck on the first floor. "How's Daphne?"

Kim smiled involuntarily; she always did when her sister's name was mentioned. "Growing like a weed. Dad's convinced she's a genius, just because she seems to recognize his voice every time he picks her up. Dad even thinks she's smiling already, especially when he holds her."

"A daddy's girl, huh?" Millie's smile brightened as the elevators doors finally opened. "I'll see you around, Kim. Maybe we can take our break together sometime, go down to the cafeteria . . ." A moment later she waved good-bye and the doors slid closed.

Kim pushed the cart toward the end of the hall, all four wheels working fine for now.

Monday at noon Kim found a gift-wrapped package on her hospital cart. Inside the box, wrapped in tissue, was a hand-crocheted pink baby blanket trimmed with white fringe. She opened the card, though it was addressed to Daphne, and thanked Millie for the gift an hour later when she saw her at the second floor nurses' station.

"My neighbor makes them," Millie explained, barely taking the time to talk. "She sells them for extra income. I wanted to help my neighbor, and I thought of Daphne, so . . ." She reached for the telephone to page one of the doctors. "I hope she likes it."

Wednesday, there was another gift, this time a embroidered sampler with circus animals Millie said she bought at a craft show at the mall when she was shopping for herself the night before.

"Thank you for the gifts," Kim said, feeling a bit awkward. Two gifts in three days was, in her opinion, a bit extravagant, especially since Millie had never met Daphne. She wondered how her mother would feel about accepting another gift from a stranger.

That evening, Carol Delaney hung the sampler on the wall above Daphne's crib and stepped back to study the handiwork.

"How old did you say Millie is?" she asked.

Kim was seated in the rocking chair beside the window with Daphne in her lap. Her sister's bright blue eyes were moving from side to side, trying to locate the sound of her mother's voice.

"I don't know," Kim said, tickling the baby-soft flesh beneath Daphne's chin. Daphne grinned; a sound, almost like laughter, gurgled up through her mouth and she hiccuped loudly. "Twenty-eight. Twenty-nine, maybe."

"Is she married? Does she have children of her own?"

"I . . ." Kim looked up, watching as her mother straightened the sampler once more. She didn't know anything about Millie Thorne except that she worked at Christian County Memorial Hospital. She didn't know where she lived or anything about her family. Millie had left the gifts where Kim was sure to find them, and then acted slightly embarrassed when Kim had expressed her thanks later. Maybe that's why Kim had felt so awkward; maybe Millie was the kind of person who liked to do nice things for others, even strangers, without a fuss being made once the deed was done.

Still, she had insisted the blanket and the sampler were enough, that Millie not lavish any more gifts on Daphne. The nurse seemed unaffected, not insulted at all. She had waved good-bye to Kim, as friendly as ever, when Kim left the hospital, the sampler tucked beneath her arm.

"I don't know anything about Millie Thorne," Kim told her mother. "She's friendly, all the nurses are. But . . ."

"But what?" her mother asked as she straightened the sheet on Daphne's crib. Daphne was still awake, though her eyes were growing heavier, her movements more jerky as she fought back sleep. "There's something that bothers you about Millie, isn't there? What? Is it the gifts?"

Kim shrugged. She'd thought about Millie off and on all evening and decided the gifts were given simply because Millie liked babies.

Or maybe she just liked surprising people. Mrs. Davis had a silk flower arrangement in her office Millie had given her when she'd been promoted to Director of Volunteers.

"Is she asleep?" her mother asked, reaching for Daphne.

Kim handed her sister over, being careful not to wake her, and watched as her mother placed her in the crib. Daphne's tiny hands curled into fists and she held them in the air for a few moments before finally settling back into peaceful slumber.

Her mother stood silently by the crib. "You know," she said finally, "sometimes when I look at Daphne I can't help but think about Jeremy Sweet. I wonder if he's safe tonight, if he's being looked after, fed, bathed, tucked into a comfortable bed. Every time I see a child about his age I look twice just to make sure it's not him. It doesn't matter who's pushing the carriage, whether it's someone I've known all my life, or a total stranger, I always look."

Kim remained silent; she knew exactly how her mother felt. She'd done those same things the past two weeks following Jeremy Sweet's abduction.

"I took Beth Ann to the grocery store with me today," her mother said. "She wandered off once, not far, just around the corner to the next aisle. But when I looked up and she was gone, my heart stopped. She was only out of my sight for a few seconds, Kim, but in those few seconds I experienced the terror, the helplessness that Jeremy's family has had to live with since his disappearance."

Kim looked up after a few seconds. Her mother was watching Daphne, and Kim saw reflected in her mother's eyes the same love, the same overprotectiveness she'd felt for Daphne since the night of the murders. It was one of the reasons she didn't like Miss Chancellor, one of the reasons she'd been reluctant to accept Millie's gifts. They were both strangers who were trying to get close to Daphne.

"I find it hard to trust people after something like this happens," her mother said. "And that's really not fair. There are a lot of people like Millie Thorne, people who love babies, no matter who they belong to. There's something about a newborn that brings out a maternal instinct in most women, young or old. Let's not let what happened to the Sweets scare us so much that we can't see people for who they really are."

"Like Millie Thorne?"

Her mother smiled. "Actually I was thinking about Miss Chancellor and Millie. I doubt Millie has children of her own. Otherwise she'd buy things to keep, not give away. She's at an age where most women start thinking about starting a family of their own, if they haven't already." She wrapped her arm around Kim's waist and walked with her to the door, switching off the overhead bulb, leaving the nursery swathed in soft, golden light from a night light against the wall. "Miss Chancellor can't have children of her own. And it's a shame because she loves them so much."

"Younger children maybe," Kim said. "Not teenagers."

They reached the top of the stairs and her mother leaned against the banister. "My point is, I know you worry about Daphne. We all do. But don't let what happened to Jeremy Sweet keep you from making friends. Millie sounds lonely; she might need a friend too."

Kim nodded, and later that night, when she crawled into bed, she decided to make an effort to get to know Millie Thorne better. She'd invite her to the cafeteria for a glass of iced tea and she'd find out everything she needed to know. Where did Millie live? Was she married? Did she have children? After all, a good reporter knew exactly which questions to ask so a person would talk freely about themselves.

Six

"My parents split up before I was born. I never knew my dad." Millie was seated across the table from Kim, her blond hair plaited into a single braid, the way it always was when she was on duty. They'd decided to come to the cafeteria instead of the employee break room because it was less crowded and they could talk without having to shout. "Mom and I lived in a trailer park until I was twelve years old. She worked as a waitress at a truck stop. When I was twelve, she fell in love again, married, and went on the road. I was sent to live with my grandmother."

Kim drank her iced tea silently. Once Millie had begun to talk about herself, supplying details about her past, she'd needed little prompting to continue. She often paused between sentences, staring off into space, gathering her thoughts.

"Grandma was a sweet woman. We lived in

the country until I was sixteen. By then her health had started to fail so we moved to town. I was much happier." Millie swirled her tea so the ice clinked against the sides of the glass. "Not happy, mind you. But happier."

"Why weren't you happy?" Kim asked.

Millie smiled, the way she had throughout their conversation. "I was living in a house with a woman in her sixties, a woman whose eyesight was starting to fail, whose aches and pains prevented her from doing the things she'd always done. Cooking. Cleaning. Gardening. Eventually it got where Grandma couldn't even go shopping. So I started doing all the things she couldn't."

Millie was staring off into space again.

"I wasn't happy because I was lonely," she said after a few seconds. "Not that Grandma wasn't good company. She tried. She wanted to teach me how to crochet, knit, cook; all the things she loved. But I never learned." She laughed and finished her tea. "That's why I had to buy Daphne's gifts. Grandma said I was too restless to learn handiwork."

"Where did you and your grandmother live?" Kim asked.

"Idaho. My mother and stepfather visited occasionally. Not often; they never stayed for more than a few days. My grandmother died when I was eighteen, the summer after I graduated high school. It was then I decided to become a nurse. Though I never thought I'd wind up working in the nursery. I always thought I'd care for older people, the terminally ill, the way I looked after my grandmother." Millie glanced at her watch, pushed her chair back and prepared to return upstairs.

"What about your mother?"

"She's still married. Her husband retired a few years ago. They live near the ocean, happy as can be."

"Do you ever see her?" Kim grabbed her purse from the back of her chair and prepared to follow Millie back to work.

Millie shook her head. She glanced at her watch again. "I have to get back, Kim. My supervisor doesn't like it if I'm late."

"How'd you wind up in Oklahoma?" Kim asked as they left the cafeteria and walked toward the elevators. "Do you have family in New Testament?"

"No." Millie jabbed the button. "And that's precisely why I'm here. After my grandmother died, I knew I'd never depend on anyone again. I visited my mother for a while. But it wasn't the same, you know. She has her own life. It's time I have mine." Millie stepped into the elevator and rode silently to the second floor. Just before the door opened again, she turned to Kim. "Thanks for inviting me to share your break. And thanks for showing me a picture of Daphne. She's really cute."

Kim touched her purse; her wallet was nestled in the bottom. She'd brought a photograph of Daphne, the one taken at the hospital the night she was born, especially to show Millie.

She was glad now she'd remembered their earlier conversation, when Millie had asked to see a picture.

"I've tried making friends with my co-workers." Millie picked up the conversation again on her own. "But I don't seem to have very much in common with any of them. The ones who are married talk about their spouses, their children. The single ones talk about their social lives, who they're dating, the hottest clubs in town. I don't go because I don't drink, and I don't dance, especially to country and western."

"What do you do?" Kim asked.

"Stay home, mostly. I go to the movies on my days off. Sometimes I go shopping afterward." Millie held the door open a moment longer before stepping off on the second floor. "Maybe you'd like to go with me sometime? There's the neatest little shop in the mall just for children. I think about you and Daphne every time I go in."

"Sure." Kim rode to the top floor alone without setting a definite date to go to shopping with Millie. She liked the young nurse, especially now after they'd had a chance to talk. Millie was lonely, that much was apparent. But she'd talked about herself openly and honestly, not once complaining because she'd been sent to live with her grandmother, or that she'd had to care for her grandmother during a lengthy illness. Millie loved her work, she'd said so herself several times. She fell in love with all the newborns and often wondered what happened to them once they left the hospital. That's why she'd taken a special interest in Daphne, why she'd gone out of her way to buy her gifts.

Kim stored her purse in the storage closet and pushed the cart out into the hall. It was two-thirty, time to continue her rounds.

By four o'clock, she'd replenished her supply of magazines with new, updated editions and hung her smock inside the closet. Millie stopped by as Kim was locking the door.

"I was wondering . . . I'm off this weekend. Would you like to see a movie?"

Kim hesitated, running through her thoughts quickly. She'd planned to take Daphne to the park, had promised to take Beth Ann to the library, and she had hoped to spend some time with Debra, but her best friend was going to be out of town visiting relatives.

"Sunday?" Kim asked. That would give her time to do everything she wanted to do and still make plans with Millie.

"Sunday's fine. There's a matinee at the theater on James Street. Give me your number. I'll call you tomorrow, we'll set up a time to meet."

Kim scribbled her telephone number on a scrap of paper from her purse. "See you Sunday," she said, as she watched Millie retreat down the hall.

That evening, just before dinner, her mother announced plans for a family cookout Sunday afternoon.

"Your dad's invited several major advertisers hoping to convince them to take out larger ads in the *Script*." Her mother looked up from setting the table. "I'm sorry to ruin your plans with Millie." She went to the stove where Miss Chancellor had baked a casserole and a loaf of french bread and left them warming in the oven. "You know," she said as she slipped the mitts over her hands and carried the steaming dish back to the table, "you could always invite Millie here Sunday. I could introduce her to Lee Buckner from the auto parts store downtown. He's always stopping by the office, complaining because he can't meet a nice woman. And there's always Uncle Dare, though I doubt he'll attend . . ."

Kim laughed as she helped her mother carry glasses of iced tea to the table. Her mother the matchmaker; she'd have to remember to tell Millie the invitation included introductions to several of New Testament's most eligible bachelors.

Millie called the next day, just past one o'clock, and accepted the Delaneys' invitation without hesitation. She ended the conversation quickly, saying she had to go shopping for a new outfit.

Sunday morning Kim awoke in a good mood, if for no other reason because it was Miss Chancellor's day off and she could go padding into Daphne's room without having to worry about the door being locked.

Kim was disappointed to find her sister's crib empty. She was no doubt downstairs with Tim or her mother or father, feeding on her bottle, anxious to be rocked back to sleep once she was finished.

Kim showered, slipped on a pair of jeans and T-shirt and headed downstairs to help her mother in the kitchen. She smelled the aroma of barbecue sauce and baked beans the moment she reached the bottom of the stairs.

Barbara Chancellor was in the kitchen, stirring a pot with a wooden spoon when Kim entered the room. She looked up, but went right back to work without speaking. Daphne was seated in her baby carrier on the kitchen table watching Miss Chancellor work.

"What are you doing here?"

"Your mother invited me." Miss Chancellor went to the refrigerator and removed a head of lettuce from the crisper. "Make yourself useful, Kim. We need a tossed salad."

"Where's Mother?"

"Outside with Beth Ann and Tim. Tim's setting up the tables and chairs." She held the lettuce toward Kim again. "Your father was called into the office but he'll be home in time to cook the steaks. I made a list of things to do before the guests arrive. If it rains," she said looking out the kitchen window, her eyes narrowing at the gray clouds rolling in from the south, "and it looks like it might, you'll have to help me move everything inside."

Kim's good mood slipped away. What was supposed to be a party had turned into another opportunity for Miss Chancellor to boss her around.

Millie arrived just before ten. She was dressed in white shorts and a yellow blouse, her light-colored hair worn loose around her shoulders.

Beth Ann warmed up to the young nurse in record time. "What to see my playhouse outside?" she asked, tugging on Millie's hand.

"I'd love to. I had a playhouse when I was a little girl. I made it myself out of scrap lumber." She followed Beth Ann outside, the kitchen door closing behind them.

Kim wished she could have gone with them, but Miss Chancellor had her list taped to the oven door, and there were still several tasks which hadn't been completed yet. Kim glanced at the clock; it was ten-thirty. The other guests weren't due to arrive for another hour.

Eventually Millie returned to the kitchen alone. Her hair was windblown, her face red from exertion. She and Beth Ann had been playing tag until Beth Ann had gotten bored with the game and gone off in search of Tim. She wanted someone to push her in her swing and Millie had taken the opportunity to escape inside.

It wasn't until Miss Chancellor accidentally knocked a glass pitcher from the kitchen counter, shattering in on the tile floor, that she spoke to Millie for the first time since their introductions.

"I'll help you sweep it up," Millie said.

"I'll do it myself." Miss Chancellor stooped down and began to pick up the shards of glass. "I can't believe I was so clumsy..." She stopped momentarily and stared at her hand. A trickle of blood oozed down her index finger. "Now look. Kim, there's a first-aid kit in the laundry room, in the cabinet above the washer."

Five minutes later, the nanny was seated at the kitchen table as Millie tended the cut.

"You might want a doctor to look at your finger," Millie told her as she taped the bandage. "I don't think the cut's deep enough for stitches, but you don't want to get it infected."

Miss Chancellor nodded glumly. "I'll manage."

Mrs. Delaney was upstairs, dressing Daphne to meet their guests, many of whom would be seeing her for the first time. Kim set about making last minute preparations while Millie chattered away and Miss Chancellor stared sullenly at her injury. Just about everything was ready except the steaks. Kim's father would be arriving home any minute. Tim already had the charcoal heated and was keeping Beth Ann occupied outside.

"I haven't met Daphne yet," Millie said.

Miss Chancellor looked up, still not smiling. "She's sweet. Hardly any trouble at all."

Daphne was dressed in a pink-and-white frock when Carol Delaney carried her into the kitchen. She seemed to sense it was a special occasion and was in an exceptionally good mood, cooing loudly before anyone even spoke to her.

Millie immediately left the table, joining Kim's mother just inside the door. "Such blue eyes," she said, smiling down at Daphne. "As blue as Kim's."

"She has her father's eyes and her mother's temperament." Mrs. Delaney handed her over to Millie and went to the refrigerator to retrieve a bottle. "Thank goodness for me it wasn't reversed, the way it is with Beth Ann. She'd cried even after she was fed and changed. Alex and I spent many a restless night walking the floor. The twins were easier to care for; they were content to eat and sleep, just like Daphne."

"I'll take her now." Miss Chancellor rose from the table and slowly crossed the room. "She's used to me feeding her."

"Millie works in a nursery," Mrs. Delaney said. "I'm sure—"

"She'll eat better if I'm holding her." Miss Chancellor took Daphne in her arms and carried her back to the table.

Carol Delaney started to say something, but glanced at Kim and changed her mind. She looked out the window, watching as her husband came through the back gate, shrugging out of his suit jacket and draping it across the back of a patio chair. He rolled up the sleeves of his white shirt and went about getting the barbecue grill ready to fire up.

"Our guests should be arriving anytime,"

she said, trying to ease some of the tension. Millie was standing awkwardly by the door; Kim was staring at her mother, wishing she'd say something to Miss Chancellor, but knowing she wouldn't. "Come on, Millie. There's someone I want you to meet. He's—"

Kim lingered in the kitchen for a few minutes after her mother and Millie went outside. Miss Chancellor was feeding Daphne, oblivious to anyone else around her. She rocked back and forth in the chair, humming a lullaby, her eyes fixed dreamily on Daphne's soft expression.

Daphne stared up at her as the nanny removed the bottle from her mouth and wiped a trace of formula from her chin. Daphne burped a small burp.

"That's a good girl."

Daphne cooed; she raised her hands toward the bottle and Miss Chancellor continued to feed her. A moment later, the lullaby continued, barely audible above the voices that came from the patio.

Millie went home at six o'clock; Kim was the only one who noticed she stayed away from Miss Chancellor for the rest of the day.

"Soon," she whispered. "Very soon you'll have a sister."

She bathed him in a plastic tub by the kitchen sink and wrapped him in a plush white towel afterward.

Jeremy Don was in an especially playful mood; he seemed to like the water.

68

She looked forward to warmer weather when they could take a vacation together, just the three of them.

Maybe they'd go to the beach.

"You'd like that, wouldn't you, baby?"

Jeremy Don responded, not with a smile; he watched her as she carried him around the room, his eyes alert, full of curiosity.

"Mommy," she said, pointing to herself.

He turned his head and looked away.

She could call herself Mommy all she wanted, but that didn't make it so.

She laid him on the mattress and sat beside him, tickling his stomach. But he wouldn't smile again. Before long he drifted off to sleep. She considered leaving him alone to rest, but decided she wanted to be close to him.

If he was content to sleep, she would be content to hold him.

So she lifted him gently into her arms and carried him to the chair beside the window.

Twenty minutes passed.

"Hush, little baby, don't you cry."

The house was dark an hour later.

"Momma's gonna buy you a mockingbird."

She didn't move, not even to rock the chair.

"If that mockingbird don't sing . . ."

She could no longer see his face, merely a a silhouette of his tiny, perfect features in the twilight.

"Momma's gonna buy you a . . ."

He became restless, kicking his legs at the soft, whispered sound of her voice. She wished she knew what he was dreaming, what he was thinking.

69

Was he lonely, as lonely as she was? Did he know what she was planning? Did he understand what she had been telling him, that soon there would be another baby, a sister?

Of course not. Jeremy was only a baby himself. Too young to understand her intentions. But someday, when he was older, he'd know, he'd understand. What she was going to do—what she had to do—was as much for his sake as her own. It wasn't fair, rasing a child alone. Children needed siblings; how else would they learn to share, to care about someone other than themselves?

If only he'd smile again, just once more, so she'd know what she'd done—what she was going to do— was worth it.

"Soon," she whispered, and thought of Daphne, and all the people who were going to try and stop her. Jeremy needed a sister; she needed a daughter. Didn't they understand that?

She sat for hours, cradling Jeremy, and making plans.

Seven

The next day at the hospital, Millie handed Kim a shopping bag as soon as she stepped off the elevator.

"Tell your mother thank-you for yesterday. I really enjoyed myself."

Inside the bag, wrapped in tissue, were two teddy bears, one with a red bow for Beth Ann, the other a pink bow, for Daphne.

"I wish she didn't feel she had to buy so many gifts," Carol Delaney said that evening over dinner.

Beth Ann went to sleep that night clutching her bear; Daphne's was at the foot of her crib.

Tuesday morning, Kim drove to the *Daily Script* at her father's request and set about helping Mrs. Pease edit the new ads that had come in after the family barbecue. Her father was going to be out of town all day, and her mother, for once, decided to stay home and rest and let Kim help in the office.

Just before noon Kim took several new subscriptions over the telephone, typed the information into the computer and printed out a master list of upcoming renewals.

"I'm going across the street to order lunch," Mrs. Pease said standing in front of Kim's desk, her glasses draped around her neck on a strand of black beads. "What would you like to eat?"

Kim placed her order and wandered toward the back to her mother's office. The phones were quiet for the first time all day, and she was the only one in the office. Her mother's desk, as always, was organized into tiny piles of information. Manila folders held future stories, follow-up stories, and human interest stories for those days when there wasn't enough hard-hitting news to fill the pages of the *Script*.

Kim sat behind her mother's desk to wait for Mrs. Pease's return. There was no need to start another project until after lunch. She could see any customers who came in through the front door from the window in her mother's office.

Carol Delaney was working on an editorial outlining the city's new tax proposal. Kim scanned her mother's notes quickly; as scant as they were, Kim knew was mother was opposed to the proposal for various reasons, mainly because not enough money had been set aside for summer youth programs.

Kim was about to return to the front of the office when she noticed a file folder labeled B. Chancellor on the corner of the desk. This was her mother's file, and as much as Kim was tempted, she knew she shouldn't pry into her mother's personal property. Still she was curious. What kind of information did her mother have on Miss Chancellor? Kim had seen the nanny's resumé; but was there more, some new information that might make her feel differently about Miss Chancellor? She wanted to like Miss Chancellor, to trust her; after all she was Beth Ann and Daphne's caretaker.

Opening the file folder, she read quickly, looking up occasionally to make sure Mrs. Pease wasn't about to return and catch her snooping through her mother's papers. There was nothing Kim hadn't seen before. Miss Chancellor's resumé, her letters of recommendation, the agency contract signed by both parties. Carol Delaney had written several notes while talking to Miss Chancellor's past employers. She was highly praised, called everything from wise and wonderful to sweet and sentimental.

"Are we talking about the same woman here?" Kim muttered aloud.

It wasn't until she reached the last page of her mother's notes that she saw a notation circled heavily in black ink.

See wire story dated this year, January 15. *Daily Script*, page 2.

Kim slid the folder back where she'd found it and went immediately to the storeroom where copies of the *Daily Script* were stacked in order of publication, according to date. The morgue was almost as large as the outer offices, and though it was dimly lit and smelled of musty newspaper, this was Kim's favorite place to work. She loved reading about New Testament's history, especially those years when the newspaper had been the *Daily Scripture*.

January 15th. Page two.

She found the edition she wanted and spread it open on the work table.

"Oklahoma City Woman Cleared of Abduction Charges."

She was still staring at the headline a few minutes later when Mrs. Pease returned with lunch.

At three o'clock, Kim left the newspaper office and headed home over the Psalm River Bridge. She played the radio and drummed her fingers against the steering wheel as she drove. Still, the actions did little to solve the questions that raced through her mind. There had to be a logical explanation; her mother wouldn't have lied to her—wouldn't have kept something so important a secret—without a reason.

She had promised to stay at the *Script* for as long as Mrs. Pease needed her. Thankfully, things had slowed down by two-thirty; a few minutes before three, Mrs. Pease told Kim to go home, that she'd helped a lot, but it was obvious she had other things on her mind.

She had to get home and talk to her mother, to find out the truth about Miss Chancellor and the boy she had been accused of abducting.

Her mother's car wasn't parked in front of the garage when Kim finally reached Jude Drive and steered her car into the driveway. But Miss Chancellor's was.

The front door was locked. Kim fumbled for her keys. Before the Sweets' murders people in New Testament rarely locked their doors. But everything had changed since that night. People were suspicious of their friends, family, and neighbors. Kim was no exception.

The house was empty when she stepped into the foyer—too quiet for anyone to be home.

"Mom? Miss Chancellor?"

Her voice echoed through the rooms.

Tim was at the police station working with Rosy Baxter; her father, of course, was out of town, and would be until well after dark.

"Beth Ann?"

Kim went directly to the kitchen. Her mother always left a note if she went somewhere and there was no one home to tell what time she'd be returning. It was one of Carol Delaney's strict rules; even as lax as she seemed with Miss Chancellor sometimes, she insisted the nanny leave a note if she left the house, even for a few minutes.

But there was no note.

Kim stood beside the kitchen counter for a moment, trying to slow her pounding heart, trying not to let her thoughts race with all kinds of possibilities. Bad possibilities. Just because she'd read the article about Miss Chancellor, just because she'd been thinking about the Sweets minutes earlier, didn't mean there was anything wrong.

There was no need to panic.

Still, she raced upstairs, calling her mother's name with every step.

Daphne was not in her nursery; not that Kim had expected her to be. She stood inside the door, staring at the empty crib.

Perhaps she had overlooked a note—it wasn't like her mother to leave home without telling someone where she could be located—so she returned to the kitchen and searched the counters again. Nothing near the telephone. Nothing on her mother's desk. Nothing taped to the laundry room wall.

She called the *Daily Script*. Mrs. Pease answered on the second ring.

"Did my mother call after I left?" Kim asked, trying to keep the worry from her voice.

"No," Mrs. Pease said. "I haven't talked to your mother today. Is there something wrong?"

"No one called for me, right?"

"No one. Kim, is there something the matter?"

"There's . . ." She wondered if she was over-reacting, about to worry Mrs. Pease needlessly. "There's no one home, Mrs. Pease and, I don't know where Beth Ann and Daphne are. I don't know where anyone is."

She wouldn't have been so frightened if she hadn't read the article that afternoon. Miss Chancellor was innocent; she'd read the

76

words herself, in black and white. But there was always the possibility. . . .

She'd been left in charge of Beth Ann and Daphne that morning. She could have kidnapped them and driven to another state by now.

That only left one question—where was Kim's mother?

"I'm sure everything's okay," Mrs. Pease said, her voice no longer that of a newspaper employee, but a friend. "Why don't you get in your car and drive around the neighborhood? It's a beautiful day outside. Your mother might have taken the girls to the park."

"She always leaves a note. Always."

"Maybe she forgot, just this once. If you don't find them in ten minutes, call me back. We'll decide what to do next."

"Okay." Kim dropped the telephone back into the receiver, grabbed her keys and headed outside. She tried to remain calm as she started her car and drove down Jude Drive again. The park was just a few blocks away.

Her hands were trembling by the time she turned the first corner.

Kim's temples throbbed as she strained to see through the windshield. The tree-lined avenue that led to the neighborhood park was just ahead. There were several children playing on the grass, some tossing Frisbees, others racing toward the swings and seesaws.

None of them looked familiar.

She'd reached the park entrance when she

finally saw a tumble of brown hair and heard Beth Ann's high-pitched squeal through her open window. Kim pulled to the curb, not caring if she was parked between the yellow lines, and shoved open the door.

Beth Ann spotted her and waved. "Daphne loves the—"

Kim dropped to her knees and hugged her sister so tightly Beth Ann began to protest at once. "Stop it! You're hurting me!"

"Sorry." Kim reached out and touched her sister's flushed cheek. "Who brought you here? Where's Mom?"

"She went to the doctor—"

"The doctor! Why?"

"She drove Miss Chancellor." Millie Thorne pushed Daphne's stroller through the soft grass toward Kim. Daphne was asleep, her head lolled to one side, away from the sun. Millie was smiling, obviously unaware that she'd scared the daylights out of Kim. "What are you doing here?" she asked, parking the stroller and kneeling down to make certain Daphne was all right.

"I came home. There was no one there. I was worried." Kim sat on the grass and let her heart slow to its normal pulse. "You should have left a note, Millie."

"I'm sorry, Kim. I—"

"Why did Miss Chancellor have to go to the doctor?" Now that she knew her sisters were safe, she wanted answers more than apologies.

"You remember she cut her finger Sunday."

Millie, satisfied that Daphne was going to continue to sleep comfortably, sat on the grass beside Kim and hugged her knees. "It wasn't healing the way she thought it should. The only time the doctor could see her was today at two-thirty. She wanted to drive herself, but your mother wouldn't let her. It seems our stoic Miss Chancellor, the woman who doesn't appear to be afraid of anything, has a morbid fear of doctors. She was so shaken, she was barely able to walk to the car." Millie laughed and leaned back so her face was bathed in sunlight. "I'll bet she thinks twice before she picks up broken glass again."

"Let's play on the merry-go-round." Beth Ann tugged her sister's hand.

"In a minute," Kim promised, then turned her attention back to Millie. "How'd you wind up watching the girls?"

"I happened to phone while your mother was trying to decide what to do. I called to talk to you, to tell you there's a new Tom Cruise movie starting this weekend if you're interested." Millie turned around, facing Kim, fully aware for the first time just how shaken Kim had been. "Your mother was going to ask you to come home. I volunteered to come over instead."

"I thought you had to work today."

Millie studied the tips of her sneakers. "I called in sick. I told my supervisor I'd probably be well enough to come in later tonight." She looked up, embarrassed that she'd been caught in a lie. "I'm sorry if I scared you, Kim. When your mother and Miss Chancellor left, I asked Beth Ann what she wanted to do. She said play in the park. I never thought about leaving a note."

"It's okay," Kim said.

Beth Ann was still tugging at her arm.

"You're worried because of what happened to that little boy a few weeks back, aren't you?" Millie shook her head, her expression suddenly serious. "I'm sorry. I never thought." She reached out and touched Kim's hand. "I was just so excited when your mother agreed to let me watch Daphne and Beth Ann, I wanted to do whatever it took to keep Beth Ann happy so your mother might ask me again sometime."

"Merry-go-round," Beth Ann said, peeved.

"I love children, all children. I'd never do anything to harm your sisters."

"I know," Kim said, standing and brushing grass from her jeans. "Ever since Jeremy Sweet disappeared, I find myself worrying about Daphne and Beth Ann more than I should. I can't even trust Miss Chancellor, not completely."

Millie looked up, shading her eyes from the sun. "I can't say I blame you there. She's a bit—"

"Merry-go-round! Now!" Beth Ann said, stomping her foot.

"I found out something about Miss Chancellor this afternoon," Kim said, taking her sister's hand. Millie stood and pushed Daphne's stroller as they walked toward the playground. "Something my mom knew about—Dad, too, I'm sure—but they didn't tell me, and I don't know why."

She told Millie about the article she'd found in the morgue, glad she had someone to talk to before she had to face her mother that evening and confess she had been snooping where she didn't belong.

"I'm disappointed in you, Kim."

The dinner dishes were dried and put away. Beth Ann and Tim were in the living room watching television. Daphne was still awake, in her mother's lap, looking up at the bright light above the table.

"I'm sorry I looked at something that didn't belong to me," Kim said. She waited for an additional scolding, but her mother was tickling Daphne's chin, trying to get her to smile.

"It was unfair of me to include you in the interviews and then not tell you everything about Miss Chancellor's past," her mother said, finally. "She called me that same afternoon, after we interviewed her, and explained everything. She asked me not to tell you unless I thought it was absolutely necessary."

"Tell me what?"

"I made a few phones calls," her mother said, ignoring the question, "until I was convinced Miss Chancellor was telling the truth, that the whole ordeal had been nothing more than a misunderstanding."

81

"I know the charges were dropped. Why was Miss Chancellor charged in the first place?"

Her mother leaned back, her hands resting on Daphne's legs. "She used to work for a family in Oklahoma City named Whorton. They had a nine-year-old son, Timothy. His mother said he loved Miss Chancellor very much and he was very upset when his parents decided he was too old for a nanny. For several days after Miss Chancellor left he wouldn't eat and wouldn't sleep. Miss Chancellor was broken-hearted because Timmy was very special to her, too, but she knew such an attachment might be harmful in the long run. Shortly afterward Timmy ran away from home.

"Somehow he managed to find his way across town to where Miss Chancellor had a new job. He told her he had his parents' permission to be there, and since he'd never lied to her before, she had no reason to question him. By the time the police arrived late that afternoon, Timmy had been missing for over ten hours. His parents were frantic, naturally."

Kim tried to listen with an open mind. Her mother had certainly told her what the article hadn't. But she still wasn't convinced that Miss Chancellor had been totally blameless.

"If Timothy Whorton ran away from home, why was Miss Chancellor charged with abduction?"

"Mrs. Whorton said she and her husband were so distraught, and Timmy so afraid of getting into trouble if he told the truth, that they believed him when he said he was taken against his will. It wasn't long until the truth came out. Miss Chancellor was never formally charged, although whoever wrote the article certainly made it sound that way."

Kim leaned forward, her hands resting on the table. It seemed plausible that a nine-year-old would lie about running away from home, especially if he was afraid of getting into more serious trouble. But Miss Chancellor such a lovable nanny that he'd leave his family for her? She'd hardly evoked that kind of devotion in Beth Ann.

"I can see from your expression that you're still not fully convinced Miss Chancellor is innocent." Her mother stood, drawing Daphne to her shoulder. "Your father and I have no reason to doubt what happened is exactly as Miss Chancellor and the Whortons explained it. Miss Chancellor has suffered enough; she blames herself for letting Timmy stay that day and not checking with his parents first. That's one reason she won't allow Beth Ann, or you and Tim, to get close to her. She doesn't want to repeat the same mistake twice."

Her mother carried Daphne toward the door, the conversation ended.

There was only one thing left to say.

"I'm sorry I read your file without your permission, Mother."

Carol Delaney nodded. "Next time, ask. I'll tell you what you want to know."

83

*   *   *

She carried him to bed at eight-thirty. He began to whimper as soon as she placed his head against the pillow.

"Don't cry, Jeremy." She stroked his forehead. "Mommy's here."

He cried softly for a few moments more, fighting to keep his eyes open, before he finally drifted off to sleep.

She sat in the rocking chair for an hour longer. Not until she was on her way to the bed again did she hear the first rumble of thunder shake the walls. Though the storm was distant and might not affect New Testament at all, she stood in the middle of the room, her bare feet pressed against the carpet. She hated this time of year, hot one minute, dark and stormy the next. Oklahoma was notorious for tornadoes, destructive twisters that wiped out entire communities in a matter of minutes.

She hated storms even though Jeremy came to her in a storm. But more importantly, Jeremy hated them, too.

The next clap of thunder startled him awake. His high-pitched wailing echoed through the room. She carried him back to the chair and rocked him gently to comfort him.

"Hush, little baby, don't you cry."

The first drops of rain splattered against the window. Lightning flashed brightly outside the closed curtains, followed a few seconds later by thunder.

Jeremy shuddered in her arms, but mercifully he was now asleep.

The high winds raged outside for a short time,

84

*followed by rain. Her eyes grew heavy as she lis-
tened to the splattering of water as it ran from the
eaves to the ground below. She lifted Jeremy to her
bosom and rested his head against her shoulder.*

*She loved him so. She'd known it from the start,
from the first time she'd held him in her arms and
he'd looked up at her with those big, bright eyes.*

She'd do anything to make him happy.

*That's why she was making plans to leave New
Testament.*

When the time was right.

Eight

Friday night, Kim and Millie went to the movies together. Saturday, Millie joined the Delaneys for dinner. Beth Ann was growing especially fond of the young nurse, insisting Millie stay long enough to watch the two Disney movies Tim had rented at the video store that afternoon.

Mr. and Mrs. Delaney went to bed at ten o'clock; Tim was out with friends, at the New Testament Diner, sharing a pepperoni pizza even though he'd just eaten a hearty meal at home a few hours ago.

Beth Ann was curled up on the sofa, her head resting in Millie's lap; she had fallen asleep soon after the start of the second movie.

"How are things between you and Miss Chancellor?" Millie asked suddenly.

Kim shrugged. The truth was, things weren't as bad as she had expected them to be. Miss Chancellor knew Kim had discovered her secret, but neither of them acted as if anything unusual had happened. The nanny continued to run the household the way she always had—stern, strict, always on schedule—and Kim continued to complain she didn't need someone giving her orders.

Miss Chancellor went home every evening at six o'clock. Sometimes she said goodnight to Kim, sometimes she didn't.

"She doesn't lock the nursery door anymore. Mother won't let her."

"That's good," Millie said, her attention focused on the television screen. "There's a doctor at the hospital who swore he saw Jeremy Sweet last week. At the mall, of all places." She looked up again. "Can you imagine anyone stupid enough to steal a baby, then take him shopping in a crowd? Not even Miss Chancellor would be brazen enough to try something like that . . ." She laughed and readied herself to go home.

Beth Ann stirred awake a few minutes later and Kim carried her upstairs to her room. When she returned to the living room, Millie was gone, the front door locked.

Kim rewound the tape, turned off the television and the VCR, and climbed the stairs to her room.

She wished Millie hadn't brought up the subject of Jeremy Sweet, or the fact that he was still missing. Not a day passed that she didn't think about Jeremy and wonder if he was okay. She was positive everyone in New Testament thought the same things, asked the same questions: Was he safe? Was he still alive?

She paused outside the nursery. The door was open, Daphne's crib in a corner of the room was outlined by a soft golden haze.

Her sister slept peacefully, her tiny chest rising and falling beneath the folds of a blanket.

Kim had a dream that night: Miss Chancellor was twice her normal size, large enough to block the door to Daphne's room. Kim could hear her sister crying, wailing, her voice as frightened as Jeremy Sweet's must have been the night his parents were murdered. His face flashed before her eyes, an image of the photograph she'd seen only briefly, gone as quickly as it had appeared, but long enough for the boy's bright eyes to haunt her.

She dreamed of another boy, Timothy Whorton; Miss Chancellor was leading him down a wooded path. He was going willingly, his bicycle tossed aside carelessly, the rear wheel still spinning . . . silver spokes flashing in the sunlight . . .

The next morning, Carol Delaney and Uncle Dare were at the table, both staring silently at the other when Kim entered the room.

Her uncle looked up and smiled; it was obvious he was distracted, his mind no doubt on the Sweet case.

"There's something I need to discuss with you," her mother said as soon as Kim had poured herself a glass of juice and joined them at the table. "Your father and I talked last night. We've decided to go to Dallas next week for a newspaper convention. Your father feels it's too important to miss."

Kim nodded, waiting for the rest of the announcement. She knew this wasn't going to be a family trip.

"We'll leave Friday morning and come back Sunday before dark. I've asked Miss Chancellor to stay over while we're away, and she's agreed."

"Tim and I can—"

"I know what you're going to say, Kim." Her mother held up her hand. "You and your brother can watch after your sisters, I have no doubt. But in light of what happened recently . . ." She paused, looking across the table to Dare. "I don't like going off and leaving Daphne while she's so young, but it's only for a couple of days."

"The offer still stands," Dare said. "Your nanny can stay with the girls during the day. I'll come over at night."

"And what happens if you get an emergency call in the middle of the night? You'd feel torn between responding or staying with my children because I asked you to. You're a police officer, Dare, not a babysitter."

He shrugged; arguing with his sister-in-law was pointless once she'd made up her mind.

"Tim and I don't need a babysitter," Kim said. "We're old enough to—"

"Yes. I know you are. But I'd feel better

knowing there was an adult in the house, especially at night. Miss Chancellor seems like the logical—"

"What about Millie? She doesn't work this weekend." Kim didn't know where the idea came from, only that it seemed like a good one on such short notice. Certainly better than being under Miss Chancellor's supervision twenty-four hours a day.

Besides, Millie would enjoy the company; she loved spending time with Beth Ann and Daphne.

"I hadn't considered Millie," Mrs. Delaney said.

"Who's Millie?" Dare asked.

"A friend of mine from the hospital," Kim answered. "I met her through my volunteer work."

"You've met her?" he asked his sister-in-law. "You trust her enough to leave her in charge?"

"Millie's young, but she is a nurse, after all. She should know how to handle herself in an emergency."

"And Beth Ann likes her better than Miss Chancellor," Kim said.

"True." Her mother nodded, satisfied that her children were going to be in good hands while she was gone. "I'll ask Miss Chancellor to stay with the girls during the day and Millie to sleep over, if she's available."

Dare patted her hand. "And don't forget me. I'm just minutes away if you need me."

Carol Delaney nodded again. "Thank you,

Dare." She looked at Kim. "Your father and I are depending on you and Tim to help Mrs. Pease at the *Script*. I know you work at the hospital on Fridays—"

"I'll trade days with one of the other volunteers."

"Tim, of course, will still want to spend time with Rosy at the station. You can send him home whenever you get tired of him, Dare." She stood, moving toward the telephone on her desk. "I'll call Millie and ask her to come over so we can have a heart-to-heart talk. There's a lot we need to discuss . . ."

Millie stopped by the house nearly every day that week, if only for a few minutes on her way to work. Kim saw her at the hospital; they made plans for the weekend, including a long list of activities to keep Beth Ann from missing her parents while they were out of town.

Friday morning she arrived at nine o'clock, two hours before Kim's parents were scheduled to leave for Dallas. Miss Chancellor was upstairs, helping Kim's mother carry her luggage into the hall so Alex Delaney could load it in the station wagon parked at the curb.

"Hope I'm not too early," Millie said, brandishing a bag of doughnuts. "I brought your favorite, jelly filled, and Beth Ann's favorite—"

Kim laughed as they went into the kitchen; she and Millie had joked about *pigging out* over the weekend, but she had no idea they were going to start so early.

Tim left for the *Daily Script* at nine-thirty. By eleven o'clock, Kim's dad had the luggage stowed in the back and a thermos of coffee in the front seat. Carol Delaney scribbled down several telephone numbers and left them beside the phone. She had a mother-to-daughter talk with Beth Ann at the kitchen table, reminding her that she was expected to behave, and just because her parents were out of town didn't mean she could stay up late and eat junk food.

Beth Ann looked at Kim and smiled; their mother didn't know about the doughnuts stashed in the cupboard.

Kim followed her parents outside to the driveway, taking last minute instructions, assuring her mother everything was going to be all right. Her father said his goodbyes first and waited behind the wheel, eager to get on the road, while his wife knelt on the front stoop and kissed Beth Ann. "I'll miss you."

"I'll miss you, too." Beth Ann choked back tears. "But I'll be good, I promise."

"I know you will, sweetheart." She kissed Daphne one last time and turned to Kim. "I talked to Uncle Dare again this morning. Call him if you need anything, okay?"

"I will, Mother." She felt better knowing her uncle had promised to stop by on occasion, day and night. At least Daphne and Beth Ann wouldn't be left alone with Miss Chancellor for too long at a time.

Her mother climbed into the passenger seat and waved as the yellow station wagon pulled into the street.

Kim turned to go back to the house. She'd told Tim that Millie would drop her off at the newspaper office as soon as their parents were on their way out of town.

Millie had already gone inside. She was standing in front of the living room window with Beth Ann beside her. Beth Ann was still waving, though her parents were out of sight.

Miss Chancellor stood on the front porch, cradling Daphne in her arms. She looked at Kim without smiling. A moment later she carried the baby inside.

Kim lingered as long as she could. It wasn't until just before noon, when Tim called and asked when she was coming to the newspaper, that she and Millie left the house. Kim rode silently across town; she knew she'd be worried about her sisters as long as they were home alone with Miss Chancellor.

"Aw, do I have to?"

"Yes," Kim said gently as she took Beth Ann's hand and walked with her up the stairs. "Just because Mom and Dad are out of town doesn't mean you get to stay up late." She glanced at her watch; it was already twenty minutes past her sister's bedtime.

"Will you read me a story?"

"If you promise to go right off to sleep."

"I will." Beth Ann paused on the steps,

93

looking back over her shoulder. "Good night, Millie."

"Night, sweetheart." Millie blew her a kiss and immediately turned her attention back to Daphne. The baby was on the couch, cooing and gurgling, her feet covered in white lace socks.

Millie tickled her toes. "This little piggy . . ."

Kim tucked Beth Ann beneath the cotton sheet, selected one of her favorite storybooks from a shelf beneath the window and crawled onto the side of the bed. "Once upon a time—"

"Kim?"

She peeked over the top of the pages. She knew getting Beth Ann to sleep wasn't going to be easy. "Yes?" she asked.

"Sometimes when I wake up at night, and I'm afraid, Mommy lets me sleep with her."

"Yes. I know. I did the same thing when I was little."

"Tim, too?"

Kim nodded. "Sometimes the bed was pretty crowded." She began to read the story again.

"Kim?" Beth Ann interrupted after only a few words.

"Yes?"

"What if I wake up and Mommy's not home?"

Kim tucked the covers more tightly around her sister's shoulders. "I'm just down the hall. You can sleep with me."

"Thanks," Beth Ann said and closed her eyes.

Ten minutes later she was asleep.

Kim left the door open a crack and the hall light burning. She returned downstairs to find Millie and Daphne exactly where they had been before, playing the exact same game.

Millie kissed the soles of Daphne's feet and Daphne smiled in return.

"What time's Tim due home?" Millie asked as Kim settled down in her father's recliner.

"Who knows? He's with Uncle Dare at the police station. He probably won't come home till the end of Deputy Levy's shift."

Daphne was usually asleep long before Beth Ann, but tonight her eyes were wide open and alert; she'd yawned several times in the last few minutes.

"Do you mind if I put Daphne to bed?" Millie asked. She lifted Daphne from the cushion, cradling her head as she carried her toward the stairs. "Say good night to Kim, Daphne. Sweet dreams. Don't let the bedbugs bite . . ." Her voice trailed off as she reached the top of the stairs and went into the nursery.

Kim watched television, listening to the sound of Millie's voice drifting down the stairs from Daphne's room. Minutes later, her eyes grew heavy; she knew now why her father fell asleep every time he sat in his recliner for more than a few minutes. She barely remembered Millie returning to the living room to say good night before she climbed the stairs again and closed the door to the guest room.

By the time Kim woke again, a little past eleven, her eyes were so heavy she could barely keep them open. She turned off the downstairs lights and checked the doors and windows to make certain they were locked.

Tim's bedroom door was open; he still wasn't home.

Kim looked in on Beth Ann first. Her sister was asleep, the bear Millie had given her hugged tightly to her chest.

The nursery door was open, just a crack.

She peeked in, letting her eyes adjust slowly to the shadows. She could make out the end of Daphne's crib, an extra blanket tucked neatly in the corner. Pushing open the door, she stepped inside.

She saw a figure bent over the crib; someone else was in the room.

Millie was humming softly, a song Kim didn't recognize.

She brushed her fingers through Daphne's hair; her finger traced the curve of her baby soft cheek.

"Daphne . . . Daphne Nichole . . . Daphne Nichole Delaney . . ."

Millie repeated the names over and over and over again until the sound of her voice, a whisper in the dark room, rose above Daphne's gentle breathing like a lullaby.

Nine

"Are you having a hard time concentrating, Kim? I've been trying to get your attention and all you've been doing is staring off into space."

"I'm sorry, Mrs. Pease." Kim sat straight in the swivel chair, pulling her elbows from the desk. "What'd you need?"

"I need someone to proofread these obituaries for tomorrow's edition. Here's the information the funeral homes gave us." She handed Kim several slips of paper. "Also additional information supplied by the families. Just make sure I didn't type in the wrong date or misspell anyone's name, okay?"

"Okay, Mrs. Pease." Kim glanced at the clock over the front door and set about the task half-heartedly. Reading obituaries was never fun, but today it was a welcome distraction. It was just now two o'clock, four hours before the *Script* closed its doors.

"Mrs. Pease is right." Tim pulled a chair across the floor next to Kim's desk. "You can't concentrate. All you can do is worry about Beth Ann and Daphne. Maybe you ought to go home."

"I promised Mom and Dad I'd stay till closing."

"Suit yourself." Tim shrugged and started to return to his desk. "But you're going to drive yourself crazy worrying. Daphne and Beth Ann will be fine until you get home."

"You didn't see the expression on Millie's face last night." This was a conversation they'd had before while driving to the newspaper office that morning. "You didn't see the way she was touching Daphne; you didn't hear her voice. It was really weird."

"You said yourself you were on your way to bed. Maybe you were just tired, maybe you misunderstood." Tim returned to the desk and squeezed her arm reassuringly. "Look, I know you don't trust our sisters with anyone but family. But maybe you're being a bit too paranoid because of the Sweets. First you didn't trust Miss Chancellor, and now you think Millie's—"

Kim squeezed her eyes closed and shut out the sound of her brother's voice. She didn't want to hear what else he had to say, even if he was saying it for her own good. It hurt for him, of all people, to accuse her of being paranoid. Sure she couldn't help but think about Jeremy Sweet, she couldn't help thinking the same thing might happen to her sisters.

But the truth was Millie had frightened her

98

the night before. Tim hadn't been there. He hadn't seen the look in her face, hadn't heard the sound of her voice chanting Daphne's name over and over.

Kim was scared. Scared of Miss Chancellor. Scared of Millie Thorne.

And her brother thought she was being paranoid.

She glanced at the clock again; the afternoon was going to drag on forever.

A few minutes before six, Mrs. Pease began to turn off the lights and lock the supply cabinets. Everything that had to be done to turn out the Sunday edition was complete. Mrs. Pease was as eager to leave as Kim.

"Go home," Tim said joining the older woman at the front counter. "Kim and I will finish locking up."

"Sure you don't mind?"

"No problem." He ushered her to the door that opened out onto the street. "Enjoy your day off tomorrow."

"Good night, Kim," she said, pulling her purse strap over her shoulder.

"Good night, Mrs. Pease."

Luke Levy nosed his patrol car in front of the curb a few minutes later and honked.

"I'm going to the station." Tim paused beside Kim's desk. "Sure you're going to be all right? I'll go home if it'll make you feel better."

"No." Kim opened the top drawer to find the instruction booklet that came with the new switchboard six weeks ago. "As soon as

I remember how to turn the calls over to the answering service, I'm out of here."

"Okay." Tim left through the front door, locking it behind him.

Kim was reaching for the receiver when the phone rang.

"*Daily Script*. May I help you?"

"This is Helen B. Ross."

"Hello, Miss Ross. This is Kim Delaney."

"Is your father there?"

"My parents won't be in the office until Monday. May I take a message?"

"I have a problem, Kim." Miss Ross began to explain and all Kim could do was hold the phone and listen. "Cyrus McCall—Dr. McCall, my neighbor—walks over every evening and reads me the *Daily Script*. My eyes aren't what they used to be, you know. Cyrus was called to the hospital on an emergency and expects to be there most of the night. I'm a creature of habit, Kim. I've not missed a copy of the *Script* in years; in fact, I'm not sure I've ever missed a day. Do you see my problem?"

"Yes, ma'am," Kim said, staring at the clock. "I think so."

"I walked to the corner drug. I thought I might be able to read the headlines without Cyrus's help. But the vending machine was empty. Can you send someone over with a copy? I won't be able to sleep if I miss the news."

"We were just closing up—"

"I hate to ask. But—"

"I'll be there in a few minutes, Miss Ross. You live on Luke Street?"

"That's right."

"I'll drop your paper by on my way home."

"Thank you, dear."

Kim glanced at the clock. Ten minutes past six. Miss Chancellor would have gone home by now; Daphne and Beth Ann were home alone with Millie.

Kim dialed the telephone quickly and Millie's familiar voice came through on the third ring.

"Hi. Everything okay?" Kim asked

"Sure. Why wouldn't it be?"

Kim tried not to think about the scene in the nursery the night before, the way Millie's voice had sent shivers up and down her spine.

"I'll be home in a little while. I just have one errand to run first."

"No problem."

"Is Beth Ann all right?"

Millie hesitated just a moment before answering. "She's right here. Do you want to talk to her?"

Beth Ann was on the line before Kim had a chance to answer. "Yeah? What is it?"

Kim smiled; her sister's telephone manners still needed work. "Everything okay?"

"Yeah."

"What are you doing?"

"Playing. Where are you?"

"At the newspaper office. But I'll be home in a little while."

"Okay."

"Beth Ann . . . ?"

"Yeah?"

Kim knew she was being overprotective again—Tim would call her paranoid—but she couldn't help herself. She had to know her sisters were safe until she reached home.

"You know what to do in case of emergency, don't you? If anything happens you dial 911."

"I remember. Mommy showed me."

"I'll be home in a little while."

"Okay. 'Bye."

Fifteen minutes later, Kim parked in front of Helen B. Ross's house and rang the doorbell.

"I appreciate this," said Miss Ross, who arrived at the door with her hair carefully pinned into place. She fished in her apron pocket for money. "How much?" she asked.

"Complimentary," Kim answered courteously; she knew it was what her father would have done. Even though Miss Ross was sometimes too nosy for her own good everyone in town loved her. She was like a grandmother to everyone and famous for her pies.

Miss Ross stepped out onto the porch where the light was better and strained to see the headlines. "Darn Cyrus McCall for leaving me stranded. I don't care if it was a emergency." She folded the newspaper and stuck it under her arm. "I don't suppose they found the Sweet baby since yesterday."

"No, ma'am."

"I tried to visit his mother one day. Took her a pie. She wouldn't answer the door—she peeked at me through an opening in the curtains—but she wouldn't invite me in."

"Yes, ma'am." Kim eased toward the porch steps. Miss Ross was a nice woman, always doing kind deeds for other people, but Kim didn't want to get into a lengthy conversation. Especially not about the Sweets.

Miss Ross shuffled across the porch, her slippered feet moving quietly against the wooden planks. "The boy—he doesn't look anything like his mother, does he?"

Kim had never met Suzanne Sweet, she'd only seen the woman's photograph in the newspaper.

"The boy's dark-haired," Miss Ross said absently-mindedly as she thrust her thumb in a hanging geranium basket checking for moisture. "His mother was blond."

Kim started to say good-night, to dismiss the comment to Miss Ross's failing eyesight. From the picture in the *Script*, she knew that Suzanne Sweet had been a brunette; both of Jeremy's parents had had dark hair.

She lingered on the top step a moment longer. She wanted to leave, but something, some reason she couldn't quite understand, made her stay.

"Didn't Dr. McCall show you Mr. and Mrs. Sweet's pictures, Miss Ross? They were on the front page of the *Script* just a few days after they were murdered."

"Pictures?" Miss Ross glanced over her shoulders. "Heavens no. Cyrus reads me the paper from front to back. If we took time to look at pictures, we'd be all night."

"Mrs. Sweet had dark hair; dark like her son's."

Helen B. Ross jutted out her chin and shuffled back across the porch. "I may not be able to read a newspaper for myself anymore, but I certainly know a blond from a brunette. The woman I saw peeking out the window had light-colored hair."

Kim gripped the wooden handrail. Uncle Dare had said the Sweets had never had visitors. But someone—a blond woman—had been in the Sweets' house, and hadn't wanted to be seen. Miss Chancellor had blond hair. So did Millie.

She could hear her mother accusing her of overreacting again, making mountains out of molehills. What possible difference did it make if Miss Ross had confused Suzanne Sweet's hair color?

"What did she look like, Miss Ross? The woman you saw?"

She had to know Miss Ross was confused, mistaken; otherwise the conversation— one simple comment about someone's hair color—would nag at her like an annoying toothache.

"She was young, of course," Miss Ross said. "A lovely woman. Fair-skinned."

Suzanne Sweet had had an olive complexion.

"Anything else?" Kim asked.

Miss Ross looked at her over the top of her glasses. "She was really quite rude the day I stopped by. She glared at me through the window, she knew I was there but she wouldn't answer the door. I remember thinking, how can someone so lovely be so rude? She was lovely—her hair on her shoulders like a halo. A golden halo."

Suzanne Sweet's hair had been short in her photograph. Had she let it grow shoulder length since the picture was taken? Had she dyed it? Kim didn't know; Uncle Dare would.

"Do you mind if I use your telephone?" she asked, climbing the porch steps again.

Miss Ross didn't hesitate to open her door. "Not at all."

Kim sat on the living room settee and held the rotary dial phone in her lap. Was it worth it, calling Uncle Dare and telling him about her conversation with Miss Ross? It couldn't hurt. It might help.

Rosy Baxter answered the switchboard.

"Dare Delaney please."

"He's not available. May I help you?"

"Is Marsh Hampton or Luke Levy there?"

"Is this an emergency?"

"This is Kim Delaney. Is my brother there, please?"

Tim came on the line a few seconds later and she told him what she wanted to tell her uncle.

Surprisingly, Tim didn't laugh at her for reacting the way she had.

"Uncle Dare and Marsh are out right now," he said. "Luke's on another line. I'll tell him as soon as he gets off, okay?"

"I'm still at Miss Ross's, but I'm on my way home. Tell him to call me there if he needs to talk to me."

Kim replaced the receiver and hurried toward the door where Miss Ross was waiting to see her out.

"Thanks again for the paper," Miss Ross called.

Kim waved over her shoulder. The last thing she remembered before climbing into the car were the color of the storm clouds gathering in the west.

Kim knew she was in trouble the moment she pulled into the driveway. Traffic had been backed up on the Psalm River Bridge and the storm had continued to move while she was stuck in traffic. Now, at seven o'clock, the sky was gray, thick with clouds that roiled overhead, threatening rain, thunder, and lightning. She could smell the moisture, the dampness in the air the moment she stepped outside.

But it wasn't the storm that had her frightened; it was what was waiting inside.

She'd relived her conversation with Miss Ross countless times during the drive home. Miss Ross had seen a blond woman in the Sweets' house. Suzanne Sweet had been a brunette. The woman Miss Ross saw was a blond. The Sweets never had visitors. But someone had been in their house before the murders. Someone who could have slipped back later, removed a screen from the kitchen window, and murdered the Sweets while they slept.

The drive across town had seemed endless. The more she thought about Miss Ross's comments, the more frightening the possibilities became. Millie was blond; Miss Chancellor was blond. And now the house was dark, dark except for a light in Daphne's room upstairs.

If everything had been all right—if Daphne and Beth Ann weren't in danger—the downstairs windows would have been lit up the way they always were when Kim arrived home in stormy weather. Beth Ann would have been racing to the door, swinging it open, and smiling at Kim, welcoming her home.

If everything had been all right. . . .

She moved slowly from the car, cautiously up the walk to the front porch. The door, she knew even before she tried the knob, was locked. Her key slid into place, the noise it made sounding especially loud in the quiet shadows of the porch. She pushed open the door and stepped inside. Her heart was racing, beating out of control the way it had ever since she'd left Miss Ross's house and thought about the blond woman.

Millie was blond. Miss Chancellor was blond.

She had trouble catching her breath. Leaning against the wall for support, she stared into the early evening darkness and let her eyes adjust to the corners, the shape of furniture that should have been familiar to her, but seemed oddly foreign now. The house where she lived, the home she knew by heart, seemed different—something was out of place, though she couldn't pinpoint what it was right away. She moved forward a step, another . . . her feet slid across the carpet with a will of their own.

She was frightened, more frightened than she'd ever been in her life, but she couldn't run, couldn't walk fast, couldn't force herself to do anything but move slowly, one step at a time.

She hoped she was overreacting; she hoped she was being overly paranoid.

At the foot of the stairs, she gripped the mahogany railing and paused a second. The house was silent, too quiet to be peaceful. Something was wrong. Something was terribly wrong. . . .

She moved upward, the sound of her soft-soled shoes as loud as the key had been turning in the lock. Every movement, every noise seemed to echo through the rooms like the thunder rumbling in the distance.

Reaching the top, she paused again, but only for a short time before she moved down the hall to the nursery. The door was open, the lamp on a table near the window, its shade slightly askew, cast blocks of bright light against the walls. The lights looked especially harsh against the gray outside the window.

Daphne was in her crib; the blanket Millie

had given her covering her legs and feet.

On the floor, near the closet door, was a suitcase. Several of Daphne's dresses and pajamas had been carelessly thrown in one compartment; the second compartment held some of her favorite toys: rattles, a furry pink rabbit, and the mobile that had been hanging over her bed when Kim had gone to the newspaper office that morning.

Weeks of worry—the sleepless nights she'd spent wondering if her parents and Tim were right when they told her she was worrying about Daphne and Beth Ann for no good reason—seemed trivial now that she was faced with the truth. Her fears had been well founded, the nightmares she had envisioned when she closed her eyes were no longer scenes that flashed through her mind. The stories she'd read about the Sweets were no longer just words in a newspaper. What had happened to them was happening to her, her family, her sister.

Kim moved forward again, bending over the crib. Daphne's eyes were closed, though it was obvious from the way she had kicked her blanket she was having a restless night. Whoever had been packing her things had been disturbing her, keeping her awake.

Whoever it was. . . .

Kim glanced over her shoulder toward the open door. Whoever it was—whether it was Miss Chancellor or Millie Thorne—she would be coming back soon. Any minute, any second.

Kim had to act quickly if she expected to stop what was happening.

She wrapped the blanket around Daphne, lifted her sister to her shoulder and covered her head with the white fringe. Daphne woke briefly, just long enough to smack her lips a couple of times before she settled back to sleep. Kim moved toward the door, listening, alert for the sound of footsteps in the hallway.

Her mind raced with questions, though she tried to push them back. Where was Beth Ann? Was she safe? How was she going to manage to get both her sisters out of the house . . . ?

She'd told Beth Ann to call 911 in case of emergency. The nearest telephone was in her parents' bedroom at the end of the hall. It would take only a few seconds to reach the extension, dial the number. . . .

Except Uncle Dare or his deputies might not reach them in time. As loudly as her instincts told her to call for help, Kim gave in to another, stronger urge. She had to find Beth Ann, hold her in her arms, know she was safe.

She reached the top of the stairs and moved slowly downward, hoping Daphne wouldn't awaken and begin to cry. She patted her sister's back and glided downward through the twilight, the pounding in her heart, the drumming in her ears growing more loud with every step.

She heard someone in the kitchen. Footsteps on the tiled floor. Whoever it was opened the refrigerator, rummaged around inside, and closed the door a second later.

"Beth Ann? Is that you?" She was positive she had spoken the words aloud, but the house remained so eerily quiet she couldn't be sure.

Millie stepped into the living room, Daphne's baby bottles in her hand. She stopped in the doorway, as frightened as Kim. "I didn't hear you—how long have you been here?"

"I—," Kim couldn't talk, couldn't move. "I—"

Millie nodded as if she understood. "I was outside, looking for . . ." She walked across the living room floor, toward Kim. "It doesn't matter. I was hoping you wouldn't get home until we were already gone. We would have been if Miss Chancellor hadn't been in the mood to talk. The woman doesn't like me, she hasn't said more than ten words the whole time we've known each other, but today . . ." She stopped a short distance away and placed the bottles on the coffee table. "I was hoping your errand would take a little longer. Give us enough time to leave without—"

"Us?" Kim asked, the unspoken answer piercing her heart.

"Daphne and I are going on a little trip."

"You're not taking my sister anywhere." Kim took a deep breath; her voice sounded stronger than she felt.

Millie stood in front of her, just a few feet away, her narrowed eyes half-hidden in the shadows. "Kim, you've known all along something like this was going to happen. You told me so yourself."

111

Kim couldn't believe how calm the nurse was, how shocked she looked that she wasn't going to be allowed to take Daphne without a fight. She acted as nonchalantly as if she were taking Daphne to the zoo and would return after a few hours.

"Here . . ." Millie took another step forward. "I'll take Daphne now."

"No." Kim looked around the room and realized she'd have to go around Millie to reach the front door. Had she locked it coming in? Having to turn the deadbolt would slow her down. . . .

Getting past Millie wasn't going to be easy. But right now it was her main obstacle.

"I said, hand me Daphne." Millie's voice changed; though still soft it left no room for argument.

Kim shook her head. She had to stall for time, she had to figure out exactly what to do to escape. If she acted too hastily, she'd never manage to outmaneuver Millie.

"Where's Beth Ann?"

Millie didn't answer.

"What have you done with my sister?"

Millie laughed when she saw the fear on Kim's face. "She's safe. I called a co-worker of mine from the hospital. She happened to mention at work she was taking her daughter skating tonight; I called and asked if Beth Ann could go along." She took another step forward and Kim was forced to back up. "My co-worker didn't think anything about it—she

112

trusts me, Kim—she was more than happy to come by for Beth Ann. Her daughter was happy, too, happy to have made a new friend."

"You're not lying?" Kim asked. Millie was not the person she thought she knew, not the young nurse she'd befriended at the hospital. She'd lied about so many things. "Beth Ann's okay?"

"I don't want to harm Beth Ann," Millie said. "I don't want to hurt anyone."

"You mur—" Kim stumbled on the bottom step. Instinctively her grip tightened on Daphne.

"I what?" Millie asked.

"You murdered the Sweets."

It was not a question she wanted to ask, an answer she wanted to know. David and Suzanne Sweet had died because Millie wanted their son.

Why? The question flashed through Kim's mind but she couldn't find the courage to ask it aloud. The Sweets were dead, the reason why didn't really matter.

"Let me have Daphne," Millie said, holding her hands out, forcing Kim further up the stairs. "I only have a few more things to pack and we'll be on our way."

"No." Kim's fear—all the pent-up emotions she'd felt since she'd entered the house—disappeared quickly, in their place a steely determination that no one was going to take her sister. "You're not taking Daphne anywhere."

She was at the top of the stairs now.

"Yes I am. You don't have a choice. I'll kill you if I have to."

I have a choice, Kim told herself as she reached behind her and gripped the nursery doorknob. She could jump inside and lock the door if she was quick enough. It wasn't much of a choice.

But right now it was the only one she had.

Ten

Kim could hear the faint ringing of the telephone, but she was locked inside the nursery and Millie was on the other side of the door, trying to force her way in.

"Let me in, Kim." She rattled the knob, pounded on the door. "Open the door."

Kim tightened her grip on Daphne. Her sister was awake, but thankfully unaware of the danger they were in.

"You know you can't stop me," Millie said.

It was amazing how calm she sounded, how in control, even though she had to know the only way to steal Daphne now was to make good her threat to kill Kim the way she had murdered the Sweets.

Is this how it had happened that night, weeks ago, when Jeremy had been kidnapped?

No. The Sweets had been stabbed while they slept. There had been no resistance.

"Why, Millie?" Kim shouted through the

door. "Why'd you kill the Sweets?"

She wanted to know why Millie had taken Jeremy and killed his parents, why she was trying to take Daphne now. She wanted to understand her motives, if only to accept the fact that she'd been fooled so easily into trusting Millie. But she needed to stall for time, too, to plan her next move. She was trapped with only one way out. The window.

"I loved David Sweet," Millie answered quietly.

"What did you say?"

"I said I loved David Sweet. He didn't know it of course. But I did."

Kim was in front of the window, trying to hold Daphne with one hand and open the window with the other. She could hear the wind rustling through the tree branches outside.

"I don't understand," she said to keep the conversation alive.

"I met David when he sprained his arm playing football. I worked at the hospital where his friends drove him to the emergency room."

Kim managed to slide open the bottom pane. When had it started to rain? The question was fleeting, a bit ironic that she should be concerned about the weather when her life was at stake.

Worse than the storm outside was the quiet inside.

Millie had stopped talking.

"You met David in the emergency room? You treated him for a sprain?"

116

"No, no. I was downstairs in the emergency room waiting for my ride home at the end of my shift. My friend—Lisa—she was an intern at the time. She treated David. I saw him the moment he walked through the sliding glass doors. He was so handsome. Tall. Dark hair. The prettiest eyes . . ."

The screen was attached securely and wouldn't give way no matter how hard Kim pushed. She considered laying Daphne in the crib so she'd be able to work more freely, but didn't want to take the chance. If Millie somehow managed to get in, Kim wasn't sure she'd be able to reach her sister again in time.

"Kim! Open this door!" Millie punctuated every word by pounding on the door.

Daphne began to cry.

"Shhh. We're going to be okay." Kim rocked her sister. "I'll open the door if you finish telling me about David," she said to Millie.

"Open . . . this . . . dooooor!"

"Not until you tell me about David! If you loved him, why'd you kill him?"

"I—" Millie hesitated. "I fell in love with him that day at the hospital. But he didn't even notice me. I mean, I was standing there, not ten feet away, and he didn't even notice me. All he could see was Lisa. He asked her for a date and she accepted.

"All I ever wanted, Kim, was to fall in love with the right man, the way my mother did the second time. I knew the moment I saw David Sweet he was the man I wanted to marry, the

117

man whose children I wanted to bear. But he ignored me; he left the hospital and he didn't even know I was there."

The screen . . . if only she could manage to remove the screen she could crawl outside.

"After Lisa went out with him . . ." Now that Millie had begun to talk, the words fell out freely, without prompting. "I found out his name, where he lived, who his friends were. And I followed him."

Kim didn't know how much longer she could keep her distracted by talking about the events that had led up to the Sweets' murders, but she had to keep trying.

"You followed him? Why?"

"At first just because I wanted to look at him. You know? He was so handsome. But after a few days, a few weeks—I don't remember—I kept following him because he was so . . ."

"What, Millie? Tell me."

"David was the kind of person I wanted to be, the kind of person I wanted to marry. He was so popular, so fun-loving. He had lots of friends. Especially girlfriends. Until he met her."

"Her?" Kim worked for several minutes before she realized how quiet the house had become. Millie had quit talking again. "Who, Millie? Who did David meet?"

"Suzanne. His wife. They met on a blind date. At least that's what I found out later."

Kim shivered—not from the cold rain that was blowing in from outside—but from the

sudden hatred in Millie's voice. She'd murdered Suzanne Sweet because she had been
jealous.

"I left them alone after they were married. I
didn't telephone, I didn't drive by their house,
not the way I did when David was single. I
thought I'd lost him forever. But one day . . ."

"One day, what?" Kim asked, staring at the
window. Even if she managed to get outside
and crawl along the edge of the roof while holding Daphne without falling—which she knew
was next to impossible—it wouldn't do any
good. Millie could be outside, waiting for her
before Kim had a chance to climb down from
the roof. "One day, what?" she asked again. She
had to keep Millie talking; had to have time to
think of another escape route.

"One day I saw David again. It was just a
random meeting. You know? We passed each
other in the hospital where I worked. But he
smiled at me. And I fell in love all over again.
I knew he was married. But I didn't care. I got
his phone number and I called him at home,
day in and day out, all hours, night and day.
I left messages on his windshield. I talked to
Suzanne; I told her her husband was cheat-
ing on her. I found out where she worked. I
called her there, too. She answered the switchboard; if anyone else ever answered I just hung
up."

Millie laughed suddenly, the sound of her
voice so loud, so out of control it bordered on
hysteria. "I scared them. Can you believe it? I

wanted to break them up and all I managed to do was scare them. So they moved."

Daphne was still crying. Kim rocked her the way she had so many other times. For a moment—one brief second while Millie was quiet—she felt as if everything in the house was normal. She was in her sister's nursery, everything was as it should be. Daphne was safe. Kim was safe. They had each other. That was all that mattered. . . .

"I followed them," Millie said quietly. "Each time they moved, I followed them. I'd get their new phone number and I'd call them."

Daphne was trembling.

"Weren't you afraid of being arrested?" Kim asked. "Surely the Sweets reported you to the police."

Millie laughed again, quietly this time. "That was the beautiful part, Kim. They didn't. David thought he was so strong, so brave; he thought he could protect his family without any outside help. I don't know for sure, but I don't think he even told his mother and dad what was happening. I know for a fact he didn't tell any of his friends."

Kim felt her shoulders go weightless with the tragedy of it all. If only David Sweet had gone to the police, he might have prevented Millie from murdering him and his wife and kidnapping their son. He'd gambled by trying to be a hero—gambled and lost.

Kim was still rocking Daphne, comforting her, trying to figure the best way to get them out of the house and somewhere safe when she realized Millie had stopped talking again.

"The Sweets moved to New Testament to get away from you, didn't they? But you followed them here. You followed them to Oklahoma."

Millie didn't answer.

"Millie, you—"

The house had gone eerily quiet; not even the sound of Millie's ragged breathing could be heard outside the door. Except she was there—somewhere in the house—and she wouldn't go away until she had what she wanted. Millie hadn't been gone more than a few minutes when she returned to the nursery and began splintering through the wood with an axe.

Kim jumped at the sudden noise and Daphne began to cry, her high-pitched wailing as unnerving as the sound of splitting wood beneath the blade.

"Don't cry." Kim refused to cower; the fear that had kept her immobilized until now was replaced with an overwhelming anger. Millie had killed two people—a young couple who didn't deserve to die—just because she couldn't face reality. David Sweet hadn't loved her. He probably hadn't even known her name. "Don't cry," she said again as she moved toward the door instead of away. She couldn't keep Millie out of the nursery for more than a few seconds. But this time she'd be ready. She wouldn't hide, she wouldn't back down.

She'd do whatever was necessary to keep her sister safe.

Millie reached through a gaping hole left by the axe, unlocked the door and stepped inside the nursery. She was smiling triumphantly, her hair falling loose around her shoulders and hanging in sweat-soaked tendrils against her face.

"Daphne's mine," she said breathlessly. "I told you I'd kill—"

"You can have her," Kim said.

Millie's smile disappeared. "What?"

"I won't try to stop you. As long as you promise not to hurt Daphne."

"Hurt her?" Millie loosened her grip on the axe and let it hang by her side. "I love Daphne. I'd never harm her. Never!"

"You killed the Sweets. How do I know you won't—"

"You just don't get it, do you, Kim? Jeremy should have been my baby, my son. He's all I ever dreamed about. All those months, years, I followed David around, I wanted only two things. I wanted him to love me and I wanted his children. When Jeremy was born I knew I wanted him for myself; when David and Suzanne moved to Oklahoma to get away from me, I knew I had to follow them here. I had to kill them, Kim. It's the only way I could make my dreams come true."

"It was you Miss Ross saw in their house that day. How'd you get in? Suzanne Sweet was terrified of strangers; now I know why. She didn't know who had been harrassing them. Everywhere they moved, it was the same thing. Even

122

after they came here, to New Testament, you called their house, didn't you?"

Millie nodded.

"That's why she was too scared to talk to her neighbors. She didn't know who to trust; everyone was a possible suspect."

"I stopped by out of the blue," Millie said. "It was totally unplanned. At first Suzanne wouldn't open the door. I knew she was home. She was always home. I knew because I'd been watching her. Watching them all. But Suzanne did open the door eventually. I convinced her." Millie smiled, a smile Kim recognized from the hospital when they'd first become friends. She'd fallen for Millie's sweet innocence; it was only logical Suzanne Sweet would do the same, even under the circumstances.

"I told her I was a cosmetic representative. After all, just because Suzanne never went anywhere, didn't mean she didn't like to keep herself attractive for her husband. The man I should have married . . ." Millie shook herself, her resentment pushed aside. "I'd borrowed a box of samples from one of the nurses who earned extra money selling cosmetics. I had a brochure, too. Suzanne fell for it, hook, line, and sinker. We sat on the couch and had a nice visit. She showed me her house—told me their furniture hadn't arrived from California yet—but it didn't matter because they were considering moving again anyway. I knew why. To get away from me. Then she let me hold Jeremy. I knew I had to kill them soon, before

123

they had a chance to take him away from me. Maybe this time forever."

"If it was Jeremy you wanted so badly, why are you doing this? Why are you trying to take Daphne, too?" Kim looked down at the baby in her arms; the love she felt for her sister so overwhelming she felt tears sting her eyes. Daphne was staring back at her with bright blue eyes; she trusted Kim to keep her safe. Kim was determined not to disappoint her.

"I told you, Kim, in the cafeteria . . . at the hospital . . . remember? I was raised alone with my grandmother. I was lonely. It's not fair to raise a child alone. Jeremy needs a sister. And Daphne . . . Daphne's so special. I've loved her from the start. Why just her name alone conjures up all kinds of sweet thoughts. We're going to be happy together, the three of us. A family."

Kim eased forward, just an inch, but Millie was instantly alert. She held the axe in front of her.

"Where's Jeremy now?" Kim asked. She had to keep Millie distracted long enough to escape. She had to!

"The woman who takes care of him for me isn't very bright—she's good with babies, otherwise I wouldn't trust her with Jeremy so often—but she's really gullible."

Kim shook her head. "I don't understand."

"She thinks Jeremy is a little boy named Adam Abels. She believed me when I told her my ex-husband was abusive, both to me and Adam, and he threatened to steal my son if he ever found out where we were living. She never watches television, she never reads newspaper. She just works jigsaw puzzles all day; when she's not watching Jeremy, that is. She has no idea Jeremy is the boy everyone's been looking for. She kept my secret so well even the police couldn't find us."

Millie's grip tightened on the axe. "I have to go now. Jeremy's waiting." Her gaze rested on Daphne for a moment. "Waiting for his new baby sister."

"You'll want to put another blanket around Daphne. This one's damp." Kim struggled to keep her voice steady, to talk as casually as if her sister were going for a stroll. Millie was high-strung and mentally unstable; the only way Kim could hope to survive was if she kept her talking calmly, rationally until the moment was right to make her escape.

Millie looked around the room for another blanket. Most of them had already been packed in the suitcase.

"There's one at the foot of the crib," Kim said. "Mother always keeps an extra there."

Millie moved toward the bed, but stopped after just a few steps. "You do it, Kim."

Kim wrapped the second blanket around her sister, trying not to jostle Daphne any more than she had to. Daphne was asleep; let her rest now while she could.

"Ready to go," she said finally. "Would you like me to carry her downstairs?"

125

Millie shook her head. She reached for Daphne, decided she couldn't handle both the baby and the axe, and let the axe drop to the floor. "I'll take her now."

Undaunted—and with her first priority to protect Daphne at all costs—Kim finally made the move she'd been planning throughout the ordeal. She hit Millie with every bit of force she could muster; her strength was powered by fear, a desperate need to protect Daphne. Millie didn't see Kim's head aimed for her stomach and was caught off guard. She stumbled backward, tripping over her own feet and falling to the floor. She groaned loudly; her breath was knocked out of her and the sound came out as a strangled mew.

She rolled on the floor once . . . twice . . . wincing in pain.

Long enough for Kim to sprint out the door and down the stairs. She was nearly at the bottom before she heard Millie scramble to her feet, steadying herself against the wall before she started toward the rooms below.

The house was dark, too dark to see clearly so Kim ran from memory, counting the stairs as she went. Daphne was awake again, her startled cries giving Kim the momentum she needed to keep running, to escape at any cost.

She was at the front door, turning the knob, when she felt Millie's hand against her shoulder, grabbing through the darkness to hold on, to pull her back. Kim pushed forward, struggling with the door while trying to cradle Daphne. The blanket was sliding from her grasp; outside Daphne would be unprotected against the rain.

She felt Millie again, tugging, trying to grasp a firm hold.

Kim found renewed strength the moment the door was open. She turned long enough to shove free of Millie before she ran across the porch, down the steps and through the rain-soaked yard. Her shoes sank into mud, her hair was wet, plastered to her face within seconds.

Poor Daphne. . . .

Her sister was crying, truly frightened, and Kim wished she could stop long enough to comfort her. She found herself hunched forward, trying to protect Daphne from the rain, the dampness and the chill that was running down her own collar.

Daphne's head jerked with every step; it broke Kim's heart to know she had to handle her sister so roughly, even under these circumstances, but she knew it couldn't be helped.

Soon, she whispered silently. Soon we'll be safe.

There wasn't time to reach her car parked in the driveway. Besides, she didn't even know where the keys were, couldn't remember where she'd put them when she first came home. Her only hope was to keep running, to run as far as she could before Millie caught up with her again.

She heard footsteps on the pavement behind her. Footsteps that came closer. . . .

Once she reached the other side of Jude Drive, she bounded over the curb and through the neighbor's yard; another patch of grass, this one soggier than before. She stumbled, almost lost her footing, but didn't fall. She sheltered Daphne from as much of the weather as she could as she continued to run past another house . . . another.

Up ahead, just a short distance away, a porch light was burning. She knew the people who lived there, they were friends of her parents. They'd help her, protect her. . . .

If only she could reach them in time.

She darted around shrubbery, bumping her shoulder against a tree and tensing at the pain that shot through her arm, as she ran up the flagstone path.

One, two, three steps and she was at the door. She rang the doorbell and pounded on the door.

Please, she prayed. Please be home.

But no one came to the door.

The porch light was on! The Smythes weren't home!

Millie was right behind her, racing up the steps. She was out of breath, holding her stomach, gasping for air, but didn't stop until she was blocking Kim's escape from the porch.

She reached out, grabbed Kim's shoulders, and swung her around.

Kim fought back, kicking, screaming, holding Daphne tightly with one hand, clawing with the other.

Millie shoved her, grabbled for Daphne and shoved her again.

Millie pushed again—so violently Kim's head hit the brick wall beside the door. The pain was excruciating, the shock so severe she was stunned just long enough to loosen her grip on Daphne.

Millie wrestled Daphne free and moved away, into the darkness, into the rain.

Kim stumbled to the edge of the porch, refusing to quit, though her legs threatened to give way any time. She leaned again the wooden railing and listened to her sister's cries descend into the night.

"Daphne!"

Rain fell in sheets, pouring from the eaves, dripping down her collar. The gutters in front of the Smythe house were already flooded, water beginning to stream across the street.

But Kim couldn't think about the rain, the thunder, the lightning; all she could think was that Daphne was gone and none of them would ever see her again.

Dare Delaney knew he was driving too fast, much too fast for this kind of weather.

Beth Ann . . . Daphne . . . Kim . . .

All he could think was that they were in trouble and he had to help them.

He'd radioed the station once he'd started across town and asked Tim to try and reach his sister by telephone. But there had been no answer. Tim had panicked at once; it took Dare two or three more seconds to realize what had happened. Kim had somehow stumbled across the Sweets' killer when the rest of them couldn't. He didn't know all the details yet, didn't have time to figure them out just now. All he knew for certain was, his niece was in trouble.

He'd radioed instructions for Marsh and Luke Levy to back him up at the Delaney house on Jude Drive.

If only . . . he wasn't too late.

Another corner, another slide. He slowed down just enough to maneuver between cars parked on both sides of the street before he accelerated again. The pavement was flooded, the rain still falling in torrents. He tried to ignore the flashes of lightning, the street lamps that seemed especially bright in the storm.

He was three, maybe four blocks away.

Everything was going to be okay.

Everything was going to be. . . .

He felt the tires sliding, felt the back of the patrol car fishtailing. He tried—tried with everything he had—to keep from going off the road. But he knew a second later he had been going too fast this time too keep in control. The rear tires hit the curb. He jerked to one side, turned the steering wheel in the direction he wanted to go—thinking for a moment, he'd managed to come out okay—before the front tires sailed over the curb and beyond the sidewalk. The car's front fender connected solidly with an oak tree.

Dare threw the car into reverse; the tires spun in the mud, sinking deeper and deeper with every turn.

He was stuck. No way was he going anywhere in his car now.

He climbed out, cursing silently, and began running through the rain toward his brother's house. He'd often warned his deputies about careless driving when in pursuit. . . .

One mistake—no matter how unavoidable—could mean the difference between life and death.

He could see his brother's house, Kim's car parked in the drive.

He sensed right away he was too late.

Kim limped back across the street, fighting the pain in the back of her head long enough to keep running. She'd scraped her arm and twisted her ankle. But she hadn't given up yet.

Not yet.

Millie was back at the house; she'd had time to run upstairs and grab Daphne's suitcase.

When Kim reached the end of the block, Millie's car was parked in the drive, facing the street, the headlights slicing through the darkness and the rain.

She pulled out slowly until she saw Kim, then sped up automatically, about to pull out onto the street when she hit her brakes and the tires squealed, once, the sound echoing in the night air.

Kim couldn't see clearly through the rain or the lights that reflected from the pavement. But someone was standing in front of Millie's car, his broad shoulders silhouetted by the reflection of headlights.

Uncle Dare.

She felt her breath rise, catch in her throat. She wanted to scream his name, tell him everything that had happened.

All she could manage to do was point at Millie's car and yell, "Daphne! She has Daphne!"

Millie stomped the gas pedal. Her car careened toward Dare, the tires squealing against the wet pavement, splashing up water as they gained momentum.

Uncle Dare stood stock-still for as long as he could. Finally, just before the front of the car would have struck him, he jumped out of the way, rolling onto the soggy grass.

Millie roared toward the end of the block, the intersection that would take her to the main highway leading out of town. Uncle Dare was on his feet, chasing her, just a few yards behind the car.

Kim moved forward, feeling tears in her eyes, on her cheek. She wiped them away, refusing to stand by helplessly and watch her sister disappear into the night.

She heard the other cars, Marsh and Luke Levy, as they squealed around the intersection, one behind the other, blocking Millie's path at the last possible second.

She didn't have time to respond, didn't have time to throw her car into reverse before Uncle Dare drew his gun.

"Out of the car!"

Luke and Marsh were poised beside their cars, weapons drawn.

Millie was outside, handcuffed, her blond hair streaked with rain when Kim reached the passenger door and opened it.

"My baby," Millie sobbed.

Daphne was in the car seat, crying at the top of her lungs.

Kim had never heard a sweeter sound as she lifted her sister into her arms and cradled her head against her shoulder.

"Hush, little baby, don't you cry. Momma's gonna buy you a mockingbird . . ."

JESSE OSBURN is the author of several books for young people. This is his first thriller for Avon Flare. He lives in Bromide, Oklahoma.

TERRIFYING TALES OF
SPINE-TINGLING SUSPENSE

THE MAN WHO WAS POE   Avi
71192-3/$3.99 US/$4.99 Can

DYING TO KNOW   Jeff Hammer
76143-2/$3.50 US/$4.50 Can

NIGHT CRIES   Barbara Steiner
76990-5/$3.50 US/$4.25 Can

ALONE IN THE HOUSE   Edmund Plante
76424-5/$3.50 US/$4.50 Can

ON THE DEVIL'S COURT   Carl Deuker
70879-5/$3.50 US/$4.50 Can

CHAIN LETTER   Christopher Pike
89968-X/$3.99 US/$4.99 Can

THE EXECUTIONER   Jay Bennett
79160-9/$3.99 US/$4.99 Can

SPINE-TINGLING SUSPENSE FROM AVON FLARE

NICOLE DAVIDSON

THE STALKER   76645-0/ $3.50 US/ $4.50 Can

CRASH COURSE   75964-0/ $3.50 US/ $4.25 Can

WINTERKILL   75965-9/ $3.99 US/ $4.99 Can

DEMON'S BEACH   76644-2/ $3.50 US/ $4.25 Can

FAN MAIL   76995-6/ $3.50 US/ $4.50 Can

SURPRISE PARTY   76996-4/ $3.50 US/ $4.50 Can

AVI

THE MAN WHO WAS POE
                           71192-3/ $3.99 US/ $4.99 Can

SOMETHING UPSTAIRS   70853-1/ $3.99 US/ $4.99 Can